Moments on the Journey

Love in These Times

Fabio H. Soto Salom

The characters and events presented in this book are fictitious. Any resemblance to real persons, living or dead, is a coincidence and not intended by the author.

For permission requests, please write to the publisher at the address below:

FABIOSOTOSALOM@GMAIL.COM

www.fabiosoto.com

Cover design by: FABIO H SOTO SALOM

Translation from Spanish: Author.

ISBN:

Printed in the United States of America.

Dedication

I dedicate this book to the following people. The order in which I will name them does not necessarily imply the importance that each one of them may or does have in my life and in my love, except for those named in the first line.

To God, Jesus Christ, and His beloved mother.

To my life...

To my wife and my little daughter, who has had so much patience waiting for her-daddy- to play with her for so many days.

To my sons.

To my mother.

To my father... may he rest in peace.

Epigraph

In Genesis, God created the words,

In the world, we live the stories...

Fabio H. Soto Salom

Genesis 11. 1-9

Prologue

There is no word in the English language more intriguing and interesting to me than the word –"Journey". In Spanish, we can use several similar synonyms, but the descriptive power that this single word has in English, in my opinion, cannot be achieved in our language.

We can use travel, path, route, but when we try to describe the vicissitudes of life, the learnings that the walk along the path of experiences leaves us, sharing casual, important, humorous, joyful moments, successes, as well as sad ones, failures, losses that we take as time and distance separate us from people, places, and memories, it is very difficult to find a single word to define all this as you can do in English with "The Journey".

In the course of our lives, most experiences are reduced to how we live the moments, especially if we are awake, aware of what is happening around us, if we are seeing the signs, capturing the coincidences, observing how the threads that lead us from one moment to another are unraveling.

And of course, how we live them, how we keep them, how we will remember them, or if we simply will not, because unconsciousness and above all nowadays, social networks have taken away most of the minutes we live.

In that path, we leave moments that could have been, moments that were, moments that made us who we are today, moments that changed the course of what we were going to be, and moments that took us off our path for a while and then we resumed it when we woke up.

That's what these stories are about, some moments in which people (perhaps all fictional) decided to live some moment of their lives, and my sensitivity captured it and I was able to express it in this conjunction of letters that we call writing.

The way of falling in love has changed over the years, it even changes throughout a person's life, when we think about the accumulated change of the millions of people who walk on this planet and how every day more and more people fall in love, if we could compare those relationships to threads (some say red threads) we would see how the tangle is so big that we are all trapped in a network that connects us, so the way a person falls in love begins to replicate in such a way that it affects us all.

Let's see how the characters in these stories fall in love and if that way resembles what has happened to us at some point, how their journey unfolds after the relationship, and if those encounters will have any effect on our lives. Maybe it has already happened to us...

Fabio H. Soto Salom

FIRST STORY

LONELINESS

Many people argue that loneliness is not a good advisor, while others advise seeking loneliness in order to be with oneself and find a path to know oneself more deeply, as a method of meditation, prayer, and exploration of the self. In both angles, we may find arguments to support either of the two theories, but what is true is that loneliness must be faced. Spiritual and character maturity are essential to cope with it and to obtain positive results. With all this thinking in mind, I wrote these verses:

Blessed company,

Loneliness.

Are you in me or am I withyou?

Did I choose you or did you choose me?

How do I distance myself from you if I feel you everywhere?

I do not want to leave you, I feel good with you

and with no one else,

I think about what I want and believe what I feel.

Who rescues me or who accompanies me,

do not let me fall.

* * * * *

Juan José is a great friend, he is a Psychology student at the Autonomous University of Madrid, and I am very interested in his Final Degree Project because he is working on Loneliness.

My knowledge of Juan José's work coincided with my interest in the subject. I got a little inspired and took advantage of the fact that I spent a short period of time in Madrid to write the verse and also to delve into the details of loneliness in the minds and souls of human beings. I was interested.

I called him one day at the end of May to meet up. We arranged to meet at the faculty cafeteria at 11:30 am the next day. I was staying with a friend at 127 Via Carpetana. Madrid is charming at this time of year, a bit of rain and sunny days with pleasant temperatures between 15 and 20 degrees, with clear skies.

We had a sunny morning, I got up early and since my friend had gone to work, I walked for a while in Cerro Almodóvar Park, which was nearby. I went to a press kiosk, old-school style, no social media to read the news, I sat on one of the available benches adjacent to Calle de la Duquesa de Parcent and prepared to lose some time with a hot coffee in one hand and immersed in the articles published on the front page. Some headlines without diving into the details, just to enjoy the wind and tranquility.

It was only 7:30 am and the traffic was starting to form, I took advantage of the time besides the news to study the best way to go to the University, which was somewhat far from where I was staying.

I returned to my friend's apartment, around 9:30 am, Idid not want to be late for anything in the world, I took my folder, my notebooks, and my pens, I checked that at least all of them had ink and stored them away. I always like to write a lot when I talk to someone, especially if the topic is interesting and thisone promised to be so, I make all kinds of lines, circles, diagrams, sketches, ideas come to me and I write them down, I ramble a bit with the person and then try to end with something concrete. I always want to leave with something, it annoys me to end a conversation with nothing to take away, I think that in the end, that is part of the exchange of ideas, to be able to take with you some words so that they gradually mold inside you and germinate new ideas or modify the ones you already have inside.

Finally, the best route to get to the University was to walk to La Carpetana station on the same street. There, I would take Line 6, which would cover 16 stations for almost 45 minutes, to get off at Nuevos Ministerios, which was very touristy for me, it would take me through the transit station to take Line 10 for 4 more stops and 30 minutes to reach the -Parla-Atocha-Chamartin-Alcobendas- station and then walk just a few meters to the entrance. Upon entering the university, I would have to head to Einstein Street and then take a right at the intersection with Marie Curie Street. With these characters involved, one could not think of anything but an extraordinary meeting. To the right is the Faculty of Psychology, and on the lower level is the terrace of the cafeteria, a perfect and pleasant place for the meeting we were going to have.

Sitting for about an hour and fifteen minutes on the subway platforms allowed me to get a good grip on the topic we were going to discuss. I observed the faces of the people around me, most of them engrossed in their smartphones, absorbed in anything but the reality. They looked like automatons as they swiped with their fingers, with their brains blank, without a central point in their minds and without the concentration necessary to ponder a thought and analyze it. They couldn't fix a concept or remember anything at that moment. No one was looking at me, in fact, no one was looking at anyone. Wasn't this a form of loneliness? A loneliness that technology had forced upon us? Or did we seek and yearn for it ourselves? I had several questions for Juan José.

With the length of the journey, the walk through the streets of the University, and looking for a spot on the cafeteria terrace, I still managed to arrive five minutes early, so I sat down calmly, chose what I thought was the best table, far from the cafeteria entrance and not so centered that other people's conversation would interrupt us. I had time to organize my notebooks and arrange my pens. I also thought I had to establish what I knew about the topic and what I could obtain from Juan José since his was a deep approach, a scientific study after all.

The first thing for me is the difference between loneliness and being alone. A person can be among family, best friends, with their spouse, their most cherished loved one, sharing enjoyable moments with them, or those that each one can call that way by definition, and yet still feel lonely.

It's not about being surrounded all the time by people, noise, games, attending the best party, or going to the beach and having a great time until nightfall or having the best sex of your life. It's the void of not finding inner companionship that makes you feel lonely.

How many times do we feel that the people around us are the right ones? Many times, I have looked around and felt like I'm in slow motion, I abstract myself from the scene and see myself in a movie that I could watch through a screen, and when I observe the people on that screen, I see them as strangers, distant.

Juan Jose surprised me when he arrived. I was lost in my thoughts, maybe just too much.

-Hi, Miguel, long time no see. What are you doing here at the university coming to see me? What a pleasant surprise.

-Hi, JJ.- We gave each other a strong hug after a couple of years without seeing each other. -It's so nice to see you again, especially here at the university. I really have to come more often.

We caught up little by little with our personal and family matters and ordered something from the waiter to accompany our conversation.

I asked him about his girlfriend, parents, and university. I was happy that he was doing well overall and even happier that he was about to graduate and had a job offer.

After a few minutes of friendly chat, we got to the point. -So, you're really interested in the topic of loneliness,- he asked me.

-Of course, I am, but not like you. I mean, I know you've made that your thesis topic, and you understand all the psychological and physiological research behind it, as you explained over the phone. I'm more interested in the poetic aspect of loneliness, how that state affects humans in their emotional, loving, and couple relationships, in how we communicate with the people we love. That's my interest.

-Well, Miguel Angel, you've just summarized my 330-page thesis in almost one sentence.- We both laughed out loud. -It's because loneliness affects the human psyche and body in such a way that what you mention is the consequence of managing the concepts of loneliness and mental and even spiritual isolation.

-Let me explain if you have the time, he continued.

-Of course, that's why I'm here. Please explain it to me.

-Okay, so feeling lonely at a given moment is not a problem. It just means you're human, like feeling physical pain. When a human being physically feels pain, it's preparing him to take action to remedy it. So, if you have a headache, you'll take a pain reliever; if you have back pain, you'll possibly take a muscle relaxant, and so on. You associate each pain with an ailment and can end up going to your doctor to be examined and cured of the physical pain you're feeling. Loneliness acts in the same way; it's the pain of isolation that makes you feel alone and that you need to take a course of action to get out of it.

-So, Juan José continued, being alone in itself does not become a problem because there are certain moments when as an individual you need to take time to order your thoughts, go through a grieving process, meditate on your plans, and many other things that you can do alone. The problem is when you socially isolate yourself and stop sharing your pain, that's when subjectively you're suffering from loneliness. One of the characteristics of loneliness is that it doesn't have a defined pattern, you can't say that a successful person is married, plays in a band, is a renowned artist, etc., is socially accompanied and not in solitude. In other words, people who suffer from loneliness are average people, like you or me, there is no sociological way to identify them and there is no test to say that you will suffer from it or are prone to it.

-Let me interrupt you for a moment,- I stopped him before he delved into the scientific paths of his research. -You look very excited, and I feel very grateful to have come to talk to you. That emotion shows me that I am with the right person to talk about the topic. A question that comes to mind now that I hear you, does it mean that in a figurative moment, I could be walking down the aisle very excited holding my girlfriend's hand, and she could be, how can I put it,

-Hahaha, what a good question, Miguel, me walking down pragmatic paths, and you always in imagination. You never change, my friend. Well, yes, of course. If your supposed girlfriend has that pain of isolation, doesn't know how to get out of it, hasn't sought help, and becomes more immersed in her loneliness, you'll have her walking beside you towards the altar, feeling alone and perhaps, why not, a bit miserable.

-But how to identify it? How to know that a person next to you is feeling lonely?-

-You can't, never can a normal person without the psychological tools that a specialist can have diagnose such a thing, and even less in a specific moment like the one you're asking me.

-If you allow me to continue with my explanation,- he completely uncovered my intention not to delve so much into the scientific part but to stay in the soft part of the problem. I nodded my head, a novice psychologist at last. -We're almost there, Miguel, but it's good that you know that my research has led me to conclude that there are several social and economic factors that contribute to the increase of loneliness as an individual problem. The exacerbation of individualism by the capitalist system of production and the development of new social communication technologies in the last 50 years have separated human beings from the group gatherings that were common in earlier times.

-Remember,- Juan José said, -that the population used to be smaller, cities were less populated, and people used to live more in the countryside. People would gather around a fire, on their front porch. It was a tradition to dress up and go to the plaza to talk with friends. Women would receive their boyfriends through the window facing the street. It was another way of relating that was based on the exchange with other people. Nowadays, it is completely different. You must have come on the Metro for an hour, and nobody said a word to you. Each one is absorbed in their immediate tasks, and that has to do with the amount of information we process because of social media and the internet. Everything is immediate, and that's what humans have dedicated themselves to, to the immediate. When you don't have something immediate, you go to the information that runs through all those channels that absorb you and don't let you think. That's the breeding ground for you to get used to being alone, it's no longer strange to you and from there to isolation and loneliness there is no distance.

-That's how I interpret it, that the current loneliness we experience is not a choice, we are induced to it by the factors you mention. So, are we victims of some macabre plan to plunge us into loneliness in order to manipulate us or something like that? Iasked almost alarmed and remembering my verses.

-No, definitely not, neither do I think nor does my work point to the idea that we can conclude that there is a plan or conspiracy theory to make society suffer from loneliness. Rather, it is a consequence of the evolution of technology and is another challenge we face as a society of the future. We will have to learn to be more connected, but this time not to a computer or a mobile phone, but to people, to belong. The sense of belonging is what is important to humans, as part of the nature that we are and the most advanced of the species. Just like the rest of the animals need to belong to the herd, we also need to belong to some group that distinguishes and satisfies us.

-JJ, I didn't ask you, but what you've told me points to that. Let me see if I understood you correctly. Are you telling me that loneliness is then negative for human beings, and we are heading towards something like a pandemic of loneliness?

-Yes and no. Let me clarify. As we have discussed, being alone is sometimes important and necessary, it depends a lot on the person and the situation, on how they learn and how they develop. Being alone sometimes gives us the impetus to solve situations that we cannot see well when we are with others. In that particular case, we can say that the time we spent alone was useful to us and therefore beneficial. What is harmful to the human being is social isolation, which we can then call loneliness. As I alsoexplained to you, it is not necessary to be alone to feel or experience it, you can feel isolation even when you are very accompanied. Hence your previous question about your girlfriend and all that. Loneliness has physical consequences, the physical decline we suffer with advancing age can be accelerated by the syndrome of loneliness. So, if as a result of the social and economic factors I mentioned, personal isolation increases, then yes, in your words we could suffer a global pandemic of loneliness, and this would lead to the emergence of new physical diseases. However, I do not intend to put that conclusion in my work, it is only for this conversation with you.

-It is amazing everything you've told me. I came here with the plan of validating my verses from a scientific point of view, and I don't know how to organize my ideas now that I feel that what has inspired hundreds and hundreds of poems for centuries has now become a problem for people and society. It is obvious that the sadness produced by heartbreak and the time of mourning that it takes to forget a disappointment or the loss of a loved one leads us to a feeling of loneliness and abandonment. And being in thatstate, the muse of poets grows through that pain. Recreating what people can feel to create sad and lonely verses is part of the poetic essence. But at the same time, promoting an evil that is affecting our fellow human beings now seems more difficult to me. I don't know, Juan José, but it's like you've killed my creative vein for verses of loneliness.

-Hahahaha, you arenot going to come to me now saying I owe you money for lost profits, right? - joked Juan José, and then continued despite my dismay - each to his own trade, we all have to deal with the consequences of our work.

-Very funny, you've killed my inspiration and you're still laughing at me, but in one thing you're right, I brought it upon myself. I should never have come to a Psychology Faculty to look for material to write love verses.

-How quickly you come back, brother.That iswhat happens to me for messing with someone who works with their mind, right?

We both laughed out loud, stood up and hugged each other. It had been a while since I had shared time with JJ. He was a good person, a smart and hardworking young man, and success was within his reach. It was a pleasure to see people grow around you. No matter the distance that separated us, we had the certainty that our friendship would last a long time and that meetings like this would happen again, without knowing the frequency and without wanting to guess it. We would wait for them to share progress, worries, and pains.

-Now, seriously Miguel,- he sat down and put on his scientist face once again, -I really don't want to spoil your muse, but let's close the topic with this positive reflection: we already know what loneliness can do to us, but beyond that, our job as humans is to achieve that social connection and that healthy sense of belonging to agroup or a relationship that allows us to obtain the satisfaction of being connected to a reality shared with our loved ones and close ones, enjoying the alone time that we require and connecting with restorative feelings that make us stronger mentally and physically.

-Wow, Juan José, now we really agree. Excellent conclusion, and allow me for my satisfaction, just to add something to the end, mental, physical, and spiritual.

-Yes, agreed, sorry if I missed out on that important component these days. It's not that I don't consider it, but in my thesis work, I can't mention it, and maybe that's why it slipped my mind. The professors wouldn't be pleased if I were mentioning the spiritual, but you know that I personally consider it very important, and thanks for reminding me again.

-You don't have to thank me, brother, you and I know what we're talking about. We've shared so much time together, and I see that you haven't forgotten our spiritual training.

-Yes, but that's for another time, right? I don't think your readers want to mix the spiritual with the psychological study of loneliness right now, do they?

-Of course not. Let us leave it here.

We talked about other common things for a while, we ate something because it was already lunchtime, and Juan José got up and said goodbye with a big hug and lots of emotion, me too. He had to go to a class, and it was getting late, and the farewell, like all farewells, weighed heavily in the atmosphere, difficult to handle with the uncertainty of when and where we would see each other again as friends. In the end, he left, turned around, and walked towards the classrooms on the second floor of the building.

I paid the bill, as it was my turn, obviously, picked up my things, my notes, the amount of lines I had written, oh my God! and started back the same way I came. I was not very familiar with the Madrid Metro and didn't have the resources to plan a different route at that moment.

But I walked very slowly, enjoying every step and the university atmosphere that I love so much, looking around me and trying to learn from the conversation with JJ.

The first thing I decided was that I would continue writing to solitude, it is a topic that inspires me, and although sometimes I don't publish them or show them to other people, those verses make me write about other situations.

I reviewed the conversation with JJ and learned that solitude is not good for us, it can seriously harm us, but I also learned that hope and the cure for loneliness are some of the most enjoyable activities we can engage in, and that is to embrace our loved ones, have many friends and true friendships, get involved with people, not just relate and not just be part of a circle of acquaintances, but belong to a community with shared values and true emotional and spiritual connection. I mentioned the spiritual aspect to JJ, that concept was already there, intrinsic in that beautiful message he left us. -Restorative feelings,- what a phrase, I liked it and might use it later.

I was reviewing how to write about the conversation and how to present it when I was near the Humanities Library and ready to board the train. Ready for the return.

SECOND STORY

TIME

Time is a determining factor in the daily activities of all people. It is present in every act we carry out, and what we do is always in function of it. We could even add that we rarely do things out of time. There are people who are very methodical and others who are always late, and we categorize them based on how they use their time. But how many times do we think in a day, -I am going to forget about the clock,- and nowadays it would be, -I am going to forget about my phone.- This inspired these verses:

Don't worry about time...
You don't know how much I am going to love you,
whether for a second, a night, a lifetime,
or an eternity...
Just live with me in this moment
between the abysses of the clock.

* * * * *

I was walking early in the middle of Boston Common, I say early because I was going to a Boston Pops Orchestra presentation at Symphony Hall on Massachusetts Avenue in tribute to Latin music that would start at 7:00 p.m. It was around 5:15 p.m. and I entered the park from Temple Street, crossing Tremont Street at the corner where there is an iconic bakery in the best American style. You can eat extraordinary, sweet or savory bagels there and fill them with tuna, salmon, peanut butter, or any spread you crave. At first, when I arrived in the city, Idid not even know how to order them, but then I adapted and with a cup of black American coffee that seemed to me like a bucket of coffee for one dollar, I ate them for breakfast. -Things the Americans do,- I thought.

The walk from the intersection of Temple Street to Symphony Hall via Boylston Street was about 35 minutes, but if I entered the park and took it as a stroll, it could be around 40 minutes. I decided on the latter. As I said, it was still early, and walking through the park was always one of my favorite distractions. Over the years, after leaving the city, I will remember it as the best thing I could have done, having spent time contemplating the tranquility that this park transmits. It is unique.

Upon entering Boston Common, the first thing you feel is the warmth of daily life of the people who pass through it. You can observe how each one, despite being absorbed in their thoughts while walking through the park, also enjoys its greenery and spaciousness. You see the integration between the park and its visitors as if everyone feels at the same time that it is their home and are willing to share that home with those around them. That feeling is what makes it so special and the reason why I always want to walk through it, no matter if it makes my journey a little longer. On the contrary, walking through the park makes me distracted and concentrate on things I don't usually think about in my daily life.

The park is like a living being and each one of us who walks through it daily are like its organs, its cells, forming a single living being spread among thousands of individual ecosystems with their thoughts, feelings, vicissitudes, each vibrating in a different dimension yet all connected by the same energy of peace and tranquility that it transmits to us.

Whenever I entered the park from this street, I preferred to take the longest path that led me to the Frog Pond, which in winter housed an ice skating rink, and then take the path that led me to the place where the plaque in memory of Pope John Paul II waslocated, as it was the site of the first mass in this country.

At the end of this path, you have to cross Charles Street and enter the so-called Boston Public Garden, which is the same to me as the Boston Common, and I have always felt it that way. Walking through the central part of the Boston Public Garden, you cross a bridge that goes over the Swan Lake, which at this time of year is filled with families pedaling boats and enjoying Italian Ice.

It's not possible to walk through this park and not feel the sensation of being alive, of seeing time pass slowly and realizing that you are on a truly beautiful planet, feeling your steps in a place built by our human race, but at the same time representing nature and everything that the Earth allows us to share of its beauty and generosity.

While I was on this journey and lost in enjoying the path through the park, I thought about how fortunate I was to get a ticket for the concert that day. Being a student in this city is not easy. Boston is the student capital of the United States and houses the largest student population in the country. At the same time, it is home to the most advanced institutes of higher education and also the most prestigious ones. You can also imagine that this means they are the most expensive. You can come across allsorts of people from all over the world, but a rather wealthy and educated social class predominates, so prices for attractions tend to be higher than in other parts of the country.

As part of the Activities for Students program at the institute where I was studying, they offer discounts for students on various events in the city every day. It's a very bustling city, which is why it's student-oriented and touristy at the same time. One thing I learned here is that Boston is even a tourist destination for natives of the country. Many tourists from other cities come here all year round, especially in the summer.

I'm always on the lookout for discounts for the most attractive events, and I had the opportunity to buy a ticket for the concert at Symphony Hall at a very reasonable price. The only thing was that my classmates and friends didn't make it on time, and the tickets sold out, so I had to go alone that day.

Being able to see a Latin music concert at a venue like Symphony Hall in Boston performed by the Boston Pops Orchestra is something you can't miss if you come from our Latin American countries. That is why I didn't hesitate for a moment to buy a ticket for this event, even if I had to go alone.

I left the park, crossed Arlington Street, and continued on Commonwealth Avenue, another indescribably comfortable street for pedestrians and a daily walk for hundreds of passersby who want to avoid the noise of the surrounding streets. It is an alternative to the famous Newbury Street, equivalent to Fifth Avenue in New York City, but with a completely different style. Newbury is an almost one-mile-long street with all the famous shops and restaurants that you can find in New York, but with a European style in small 3- and 4-story brick buildings that are the detail that identifies this city. If you want to mingle with people and see shop windows and enter the city's lifestyle, it's a must-see, but my mood was calmer, and I preferred to continue on Commonwealth.

Everything in Boston reminds me of Europe but passing through this avenue is like being in Paris. Commonwealth is a late 19th-century avenue with a broad island in the center with all kinds of flowers and centennial trees, and the streets on the sides adorned with planters with geraniums and tulips. The history of this avenue is like telling the story of a family for several generations.It's as delicate as talking about grandma and grandpa.

I really enjoyed walking down this avenue and quickly arrived at the intersection with Massachusetts Avenue, which was the last leg of my day's walk to the concert. I focused on thinking about the evening's program with the songs that would be performed - some familiar, others not so much - but all sure to be excellently executed by the orchestra.

I arrived at Symphony Hall at 6:05 p.m. The walk took me five minutes longer than expected, I must have gotten distracted by the details in the Park and on Commonwealth Avenue. However, I was still very early - no one had arrived at the gates of the venueand there was no sign of any activity from employees, musicians, or anyone else, so I had to find something to do for at least the next 45 minutes.

The good thing about a city like this is that there are plenty of cafes and places to eat cake and have a coffee or tea. I found one just meters from the entrance to the Hall on Westland Avenue - an Italian pastry shop with delicious Cartocci. I ordered two with a cappuccino and waited until around 6:45 p.m. to pay and walk the few meters that separated me from the Hall. This time, I found the entrance completely full, which anticipated that the theater would be at its full capacity.

Being alone gave me the opportunity to observe the different groups of people in the pre-seating area. Most of them were conversing and buying wine, water, or a snack before we were allowed to enter the concert hall. I was surprised not to find more Latin American people, given that it was a Latin night. I always thought I would encounter many Spanish speakers, but that wasn't the case. The majority were older Americans who were getting ready to enjoy a night of music.

Perhaps because most of the people were American and I hardly heard Spanish anywhere in the room, despite having walked around three times, I was intrigued to hear a group behind me conversing with an accent I didn't immediately recognize. I turned very slowly so as not to be indiscreet, paid closer attention to the way they spoke and the language, and realized they were Brazilians - the closest I would be to encountering Latinos that night, I thought.-

When I was about to continue my lonely inspection round, to distract my mind while waiting for the concert to start, a blue lightning bolt crossed my gaze, my brain and left me paralyzed, almost dumbfounded for a time that I really don't want to admit was too long, or at least that's how it seemed to me at that moment and even now, when I remember it, I don't like to think of it as one of the most embarrassing moments of my life.

Well, that paralysis lasted so long that, following the blue lightning bolt that crossed my gaze, some magnificent lips opened in a wide and splendid smile revealing a perfect set of teeth worthy of a movie commercial. While the paralysis continued, the group moved towards the door with the call to enter the auditorium and passed by me, leaving me standing alone with the entire venue painted blue and the heat of shame rising up my body towards my head. I tried to compose myself as quickly as possible, only to end up acknowledging that the gaze and smile went from a beautiful gesture to one of almost mockery in fractions of a second.

The customary thought of -swallow me up, earth- that I had heard so many other people comment on and had never experienced before, began to make sense in my brain.

To me, who always has an answer for everyone and who normally encourages groups with jokes and word games, I allowed myself to be surprised by a direct gaze from a beautiful woman who paralyzed me and not only left me petrified, but also maintained the gaze, passed me by, looked me up and down and changed the provocative gaze to one of mockery and the divine smile to an almost laughing expression of amusement.

I composed myself and told myself that there was nothing more to do, beautiful women abound in Boston, and a gaze crossing had no value beyond the personal embarrassment I experienced in front of her, which only the two of us knew about and nobody else did, and since the probability of seeing her again even in this same room was very remote, then I shouldn't worry too much, in a couple of hours the embarrassment with myself would disappear, besides, coming to the concert was to enjoy the music not in a conquering mood. With all those excuses in mind, I entered and looked for my seat, but I didn't feel at all comforted. There was something else.

I sat down passing through many people, obviously since my seat was purchased at a discount, it was right in the middle of the row. I asked permission from more than 25 people, stumbled over everything they had on their chairs, and almost spilled food anddrink on a couple, I had to apologize to each of them.

Finally, I reached my seat, thinking that thanks to my stupidity of not being able to react to the gaze of a beautiful woman, I had completely forgotten to buy a drink or snack, I would do it during the intermission, there was no solution, once again the same thought of resignation, I wasn't liking how the night was going already, in less than five minutes I had failed to connect with the most beautiful woman I had seen in years, who had dedicated me a glamorous gaze and smile, and in those same five minutes I had had two thoughts of resignation. I was unrecognizable to myself.-

Additionally, I had just discovered that the excuses I had made up weren't going to work as quickly as I had hoped. They were more likely to ruin the concert than to save me from embarrassment. How could I have let the opportunity to exchange a glance with that woman pass me by? I would never have that chance again until the day I died. I was completely lost in thought and had no idea what was going on around me.

I opened the program and started reading the content of the concert's songs. I would start with a piece by Alberto Ginastera, followed by a Huapango by José Pablo Montoya, and then guess what? A Brazilian Dance by Camargo Guarnieri. Obviously, Idid not know the author because I'm not an expert in Brazilian music, but I am an expert at letting opportunities with Brazilian women slip away. Oh my god, what a torment. This wasn't going to be easy.

Due to my lack of concentration, I dropped the program at the exact moment when the concert was about to start with the greeting of Maestro Keith Lockhart. I tried to pick it up from the floor, but I had to disturb the person on my right whom I had not even looked at since I arrived, still upset about what had happened and the difficulty of finding my seat from the left side of the row. I didn't want to bother anyone else, so I didn't pay much attention to my right in the darkness of the room. But this time, if I wanted to take the program, I had to interrupt my neighbor, or rather, neighbor woman, so I began to ask for permission to bend down and take the program that was under her seat. I requested the favor without looking at her, grabbed the program, and lifted my head to thank her and apologize again for bothering her.

There she was again, the intense blue gaze. In the midst of the darkness, it seemed like she was under the immense blue sky that covered me everywhere, in just one instant, the room was no longer dark, but rather like the ocean itself.

-Recovered?- she asked me.

In the most beautifultone, I have ever heard from any living being, it was a single word spoken in perfect Spanish mixed with a Portuguese accent that made my head spin and with a hint of English that I did not understand well at the time.

She spoke to me and looked me straight in the eyes, and I felt myself freeze again. I don't know how much time passed, but alarms went off in my brain. React, my backup shouted at me. React, my pride told me. React, my intellect told me. Show her who you are, my heart told me. Don't let another opportunity pass you by, my instinct as a man told me. React!!!

-Do you speak Spanish?- I asked her.

That is what I said. How silly of me. It was obvious that if she asked me in Spanish, she spoke Spanish. Besides, why should I care what language she wants to communicate with me in? If she asked me to speak Mandarin, I swear I would turn into Confucius himself. I waited for her response with desperation, which I tried to hide, but at least it was very dark, and I do not think she could see my panicked expression at the stupid question.

-Not silly but it is the same word in Spanish and in Brazilian,- she replied in English this time.

No wonder, I thought to myself, her Portuguese accent sounded so perfect. But she called me -silly- and I was foolish enough to rush my mental processes to decipher whether -silly- was a saying that could often be like a flirtation or if she really saw me as silly. I chose to believe the former, which put me in a good position, but then a doubt assaulted me, making me feel weak in the legs and stomach. Recovered? From what? From what happened outside or if I was able to recover the program? Tremendous doubt hit me, but as things were going, I decided to counterattack with everything I had. It was my one chance from here on out and I was going to go for it all. Something came back to me, it was the Miguel Angel I knew, and all doubts and fears disappeared because I wasn't going to let this woman get away.

-I recovered everything. The program and the hope of seeing you again, both are in perfect condition,- I said, looking straight into her eyes, deeply as my mind, body, and wounded heart were begging me to do. The darkness of the room could not dim the intensity of her eyes and that color that was engraved in my mind. She narrowed her gaze, made a containedsmile, and focused on the concert.

If a moment ago I was furious with myself, now I was ecstatic. Ido not think I remember anyone having such a glorious comeback, not my friends, acquaintances, or even myself. The concert was up to par with the venue, the orchestra, and the maestro directing it, but my thoughts were no longer there. During the first part, I was thinking about taking the Brazilian's phone and asking her out tomorrow right away. I was not going to wait. It could also be that the group she was with was doing something else tonight, and I could explore the way to go with them. It was not uncommon among students.

I would wait for the intermission and approach her. My confidence was back in place now, and the opportunity depended on me, not on the chance of seeing her again, nor on my initial clumsiness, as all of that was now part of the past. I was attentive to her during the execution of each piece, and after the first two, when the Brazilian dance began, the group became very excited, and they all knew it. She looked very animated, and they made dance gestures among all of them. At one point, she stood up from her seat, and I could see that, in addition to her beautiful face, she had a sculptural body. I felt like I was dizzy for a moment. It was the first time I felt this way with someone with whom I had exchanged only two words.

We looked at each other several times during the Brazilian dance and smiled when she made gestures with her group. I started to share the movements of the entire group and tried to integrate myself as much as possible given how we were seated. It was a great start if I wanted to go with them in case they extended the night, which was the most likely and usual thing.

The Brazilian dance ended, and a Mexican song followed, then another one called Batuque. I did not know the piece, but she explained to me that it was also Brazilian, from a composer named Oscar Lorenzo Fernández, from the beginning of the 20th century. In addition to being beautiful, she was well-educated and knowledgeable. What luck I had. I had to keep going. I never would have guessed that the composer was Brazilian based on his name.

The intermission arrived and we all stood up and went to the main hall, to the bathrooms, to buy a glass of wine or a snack. I followed her like a stalker. I couldn't let her get away this time. Besides, I would not let myself be caught off guard by her gaze or smile. All my defenses were ready, and I was more prepared to go on the attack to get a date with her.

This time I could appreciate her completely. She was wearing tight jeans that fit her body perfectly. It looked like part of her skin. I could not imagine how she managed to put them on, but it wasn't important. What really mattered was that they made her figure perfect, with long, round legs, wide hips, a rounded behind that was not vulgar, a very short waist that ended in a high waistline, and a very generous bust accentuated by a transparent white blouse that she wore underneath a gray sweater that she took off during intermission, and which matched her high heels of the same color.

To that, I could add what I had already described: large, round, and infinite blue eyes, perfectly drawn full lips with a wine-red lipstick, a profiled nose, and long, golden hair down to her waist. It's hard to describe and convey what that woman influenced, blocked, and clouded in my way of thinking and feeling.

-Carmela Costa,- she said. -Nice to meet you.

-Miguel Ángel Zeles,- I replied.

-Where is that surname from?- she asked. -It's the first time I've heard it.

-The origin of my surname is a mystery that we'll have to solve in a slightly longer conversation,- I replied, opening the door to my goal of seeing her again.

She smiled widely and looked at me enigmatically. I sensed that it was because she was thinking the same thing as me and could see my intention of seeing her outside the Symphony Hall. I loved that look that spoke and conveyed so much.

-Will wehave it? Where are you from? Can you answer that?

-I'm from Colombia. From a city called Bogotá.-

-I know Colombia. My parents used to go there to visit some friends.

-Well, well, what a surprise. So, has the Brazilian visited heaven?

-Hahahaha,- she laughed out loud.

I felt like I was in my element. I elicited a genuine spontaneous and intense smile from her, and I was back in my right mind, doing what I do best, using words to entertain and make others think.

The group approached, and she introduced me to everyone. They were nine Brazilians, all classmates at Boston University, studying different majors. She was studying Biomedical Engineering with one of her friends, Joao. I was very close to hanging out with them and being able to go out with Carmela.

We entered the concert hall again and for the next 50 minutes, I dedicated myself to listening and enjoying the musical performance of the Orchestra, not without exchanging several glances with Carmela, nodding with her when the music reached levels of perfection, and applauding the maestro and musicians standing for their presentation. It was really what I expected when I was on my way to the theater, listening to Latin music in an icon city of Americanism played by a masterful orchestra that had a centenary history in a city of very high cultural level. And the best part? Having Carmela by my side.

The concert ended and we applauded the Boston Pops Orchestra for several minutes. We slowly began to leave, and I stayed chatting with Carmela about the excitement of music and the many opportunities that this city offered to students, not only for the quality of education we received in the institutions we attended, but also at a cultural and entertainment level. She looked at me for a while, which of course, I adored, and I didn't ask her why she was looking at me like that. I felt that it wasn't the first time she had done it, but in the excitement of talking to her as fluently as if we had known each other forever, I couldn't remember the previous time when I saw that same look.

When we went down, there were not many people left in the main hall. Most of the people had left. Only the group of Brazilians and others were crowded at the exit door, trying to leave in a hurry. That was like a signal for me. It's not usual for people to behave that way at events in this city. I approached the door to see what was happening without trying to lose sight of Carmela and her group of friends, so they wouldn't escape me. While walking towards the door, I realized that I didn't have her cellphone number. A thought of panic overwhelmed me, but I regained my composure because I could see them in the distance.

It was raining very hard outside. It's not that it wasn't common for it to rain in Boston or for the weather to change in an hour, so it seemed like the passage from one season to another, but this rain was truly torrential. The drops were an unusual size, and the amount of water that was falling per second seemed like it could flood the city in minutes.

When I left my studio, I did not check the weather, but there was nothing to suspect that a storm like the one I was seeing was coming. I could not imagine how to get back home. I did not bring any protection or umbrella, although it would be of little use against the intensity of the rain that was falling. I had to cancel all the plans I had with Carmela, go back, get her cellphone number, and make a date to see her again. While going inand out and thinking all of this, people finished leaving the theater. It was incredible how Americans always manage to face the changes in the city's weather. It happened to me many times when I dressed in a sweater and long pants and left the studio at 11 a.m. I found people dressed the same, but while I continued with the same clothes, I found that everyone at 4 p.m. had shorts, t-shirts, and sneakers. The temperature rose, and I suffocated from the heat. Or the opposite happened. How did they do it?

Only Carmela and Joao remained in the lobby, along with a group of elderly people trying to leave. From afar, I could see how most of the group said goodbye to her very warmly, hugging and kissing her with a lot of affection. Apparently, she was the center of the group's love, very beloved by all her friends. However, they left her alone with Joao, who suddenly hugged her tightly in front of me, so much that my hopes dissolved in a second that seemed like an eternity. He let her go, kissed her, and left. I didn't know how to react, I was almost alone with her in that large room, and in front of us was the perfect storm of Boston.

She looked at me very tenderly, the first time her eyes expressed tenderness in that way. Something melted inside me at such a temperature that she must have noticed because she immediately changed her gaze, smiled, and ran to the door speaking in Portuguese. I told her I couldn't understand her if she spoke to me in her language, and laughing, she said, -I have to go urgently.-

-Yes, but please give me your phone number so we can talk tomorrow.- I handed her my cell phone, and she dialed it directly. I felt a huge relief.

It had been almost 40 minutes since the concert ended, and they closed the doors. We stayed outside under the theater's cornice.

-Where are you going? What route do you have?- I spoke loudly so she could hear me over the noise of the rain.

-I have to take two buses to get home, I live quite far away.

-Okay, let me see how the bus system is doing. Do you know the routes?

-Yes.

She gave me the bus numbers she had to take. Meanwhile, the rain did notcalm down, it got worse, and the theater's cornice no longer protected us, and we were getting wet at an impressive speed. I searched online in the city's transportation service for the availability of the buses she had to take that were heading to the Newton area, and what I found paralyzed me. I had no way of telling her that the service was suspended because there was a flood alert for that area.

-You can't go home by bus, they're suspended.- It had the effect I feared, her eyes had an expression between pain and fear. If I was feeling new and wonderful things for this woman since I saw her, I don't know what I felt when I saw her as helpless and in need of help.

-Don't worry, let's call a taxi, you'll go in a taxi.

Her face lit up, and she searched for her cellphone in her purse. We were already getting wet as if we were standing in the rain without protection. She began calling a taxi service, and I did the same. After four or five attempts I made to different services, I looked at her, and she turned around with her face now almost in desperation. We got the same result; taxis were out of service in the Downtown area due to the same flood alert.

At that moment, I realized we were in danger of getting trapped at the entrance of Symphony Hall on the same sidewalk until the street flooded and the city's metro service, known as the -T,- was suspended. I took her hand, and we ran towards the nearest -T- station, which was about 300 meters away on Huntington Avenue. We ran like crazy, splashing through the flooded streets, and I stopped for a moment to help her take off her high heels. She continued running barefoot until we reached the station. We were completely soaked from head to toe, and I had to throw away the concert program I wanted to keep as a souvenir, as it was completely destroyed. We passed the entrance controls at the station and went down to the platform to wait for the Green Line train that would take us to Park Street station in Boston Common, from which my studio was about 600 meters away.

-You're coming with me to my house. We'll dry off and change, and we'll wait for the storm to pass and call a taxi, which should be working by the time we do all that,- I said to her as if it were the most normal thing in the world. Her blue eyes widened more than ever.

-No, I can't go anywhere but my house,- she replied.

-Well, there's no way we're walking, you saw how everything is,- I said.

-I really have to go home. I have things to do that can't be avoided,- she insisted.

I started to think that her refusal must be because someone was waiting for her at her house, her boyfriend or husband, although she did not have a ring or any marks indicating that she had been wearing one. But her insistence seemed too strong to ignore. I asked her directly.

-No one's waiting for me. But I have important things to do at home,- she said.

-Well, I promise we'll dry off and I'll make sure you get home safe and sound tonight,- I said.

She nodded and gave me one of her sweetest and most tender looks of the night. I did not know how I was going to get that look and that woman out of my head in the millions of minutes I had ahead of me in life.

We took the train and did not sit down; we were too wet. With the rush to get to the station, the conversation about how she was going to get home that same night, and her terrified expression, wedid not realize that the rain had caused the temperature to drop abruptly. We went from a pleasant 15-16 degrees Celsius to almost 2-3 degrees. The cold was chilling with the humidity of our clothes.

When we got on the train, the heating wasn't on yet, and the air conditioning was still running, so the sudden cold made us move closer to each other and almost embrace. It was the first time I felt her body so close, and despite the cold and the wetness, the sensation of warmth that invaded my body made me forget everything. We arrived at the next station while my head rested on her shoulder, and I savored the scent of her hair.

We got off and, walking quickly in the cold, we arrived at the exit of the station hoping that the rain had stopped, only to realize that on this side of the city it was raining harder, and a thunderstorm was beginning, making the journey more dangerous.

We were already very wet, so we looked at each other, took hands and started our race again. This time it was different, we were not running urgently to get anywhere, we were running to enjoy the water, to splash on the streets and, holding hands, we stopped and hugged to let the rain soak us completely.

We did this several times on the way, we seemed like preschool children playing in the rain. When we arrived at the building where I lived, I could not find the key because my pockets were so wet, and when I finally found it, everything was so damp that it was hard to open. She was smiling while drops of water fell on her head like explosions and I could not hear anything she said while teasing my ability to find the key and open the door. We ran up the four floors to my studio.

I opened the door and said, -Ta-da! Welcome!- Suddenly everything changed, and we realized that she was too wet, she was carrying her shoes in her hand and her completely soaked bag was hanging from her shoulder, making everything inside it potentially unusable. She looked at me, looked at herself, and made a gesture as if she were about to cry.

-Carmela, don't panic, please. We will solve this. I told you the first thing was to make sure you were safe and dry. What we're going to do is get you some clothes so you can change, and we'll dry your clothes. The laundry is downstairs in this building, there's a washer and dryer, so don't worry. It'll take about half an hour to wash and dry, then you can change, we'll call a taxi, and you'll be home in an hour at most.

-Men always solve everything so easily. Can't you see how ruined I am? I'm very wet and hideous.- She finished the sentence with a beautiful pout of a spoiled girl.

I had never seen a woman who looked so ruined and yet resembled the goddess of the rain herself. So, I laughed out loud uncontrollably, which made her change to a fierce look I had never seen before, and I stopped my laughter abruptly, choking on it. That made her laugh.

-Let's get organized. Let me find something urgent for you to change into.- I went to the small closet next to the entrance door, where not much clothing could fit, so most of it was stored in the suitcases that every student always has at hand and that we used to store daily use items.

My studio was not very large, on the contrary, it was at most 300 square feet in which I had a bed, a small desk under the only window that faced the street, a small refrigerator, a two-burner gas stove, and a small cabinet for kitchen utensils. The bathroom was to the left of the entrance door and the closet was next to the bathroom. That was it. I did not usually have a television until a couple of months ago when some friends finished their classes and sold it to me very cheaply, almost as a gift. I didn't pay for cable service, so I mostly watched streaming.

Well, in that suitcase I remembered that I had the only thing that occurred to me that I could lend her so she could dress while I went down to dry her clothes in the laundry room. It was a sweater that I had to buy in an emergency on a trip I made to Martha's Vineyard one of those days when I went out and the temperature was around the 20s and ended up dropping to almost zero degrees Celsius at 4 pm. I bought a Boston University pullover size 3XL that was the only thing in the emergency store I entered. It was too big for me, but I could not imagine it on her. Now that I had seen her without shoes, shewas not as tall as she looked. At first, I saw her almost at my height, and without heels, she was about 10 cm shorter.

I took out the sweater and the cloth bag that I use to go down to the laundry room, gave them to her, and showed her the bathroom, the only place where she could change without being exposed to my gaze, which I regretted a lot. While she went to the bathroom to change, I turned on the heater that had been off since spring began. I particularly like the cold, but wet and with such a sudden change, we could not risk getting a cold. Thinking about how to recover internal warmth, I remembered that I had bought a bottle of good Californian wine for after the concert. The plan was to have a glass or two before going to bed.

She came out of the bathroom wearing the sweater with unmatched coquetry. She smiled at me apologetically, but what she did was exalt her fine features. Her gaze was between mischievous and ashamed, making the cold in my body disappear. She gestured to turn halfway and turned back, like in a fashion show. The sleeves covered her arms more than once and a half, and the length of the sweater was halfway up her thigh, like a miniskirt, revealing the full contour of her long legs that I had guessed before by the tightness of her jeans. But now, seeing them directly, I realized that they had been crafted like the finest sculpture. In a beautiful white that was not pale, her skin shone in the dim light of the room. I must have stayed staring and still a little longer than necessary. I didn't notice if my mouth was open, but I was awakened by a snap of one of the excess sleeves.

We both laughed out loud with a knowing look. It did not cross my mind to apologize, not even a little bit. On the contrary, I would have liked to continue contemplating that scene for a while longer. In fact, I still remember it as it happened and replay it second by second. She handed me the bag with the wet clothes, very wet, it was dripping water through the fabric.

-You know, I don't think it'll be enough to dry it. I think I'll have to wash it first; it's too wet. What do you think?-

-Yeah, it seems so, but the problem is time, Miguel. I don't think she has much time to wait for it to be washed and dried.

-Well, look, let me change, and when I come out, we'll talk about it because that rain, plus the consequences it brought, won't pass so quickly.- She nodded, and I went into the bathroom. With all the rush to get her something comfortable, I had forgotten that I was completely wet, and I was leaving puddles of water all over the studio. I took a quick hot shower to recover the external temperature. The internal one was already very high, and I put on some jogging pants and an exercise shirt. When I came out, she had already dried all the wetness from the floor, I snatched the mop from her and looked at her in surprise.

-Don't worry, it's the least I can do. You've been very kind to me, even though you hardly know me,- she said.

I thought about the best response, it was true that I hardly knew her, we had only spent a couple of hours together and wehad not exactly shared our life stories, but there was something in my mind that was nagging at me like an alarm that could not fully accept those words, which were an undeniable fact. So, I slowly began to gather the best words that could come out of my mouth, hoping that theywould not all rush out at once and I would not say something stupid.

-You're right, Carmela,- I began slowly, pausing before continuing, -we just met, and maybe not in the best circumstances. We ran like crazy to protect ourselves from the rain, and the truth is, I've seen several things that I don't understand,- I was referring to how her friends left her alone and everyone said goodbye with hugs and almost formed a line to hug her specifically. I think she understood what I meant, so I continued speaking slowly, searching for more words,-sometimes people don't have to spend a lot of time together or say everything explicitly to get to know each other well. Today, it took me just a few minutes and a lot of glances to know that I know you. There's a fiber in you that's different. I don't know anything about you except your name, but I feel like I know you better than many others who claim to be my friends,- I stopped, thinking that I had gone too far, but she looked at me with her blue eyes, even clearer than before, and lowered thema little, accepting what I had said.

There was silence between us and neither of us reacted until a few seconds later. I took her hand and sat her on the bed, which, aside from the chair at my desk, was the only place my visitors could sit. I took the chair for myself and sat in front of her.

-I'm very worried,- she said. -We haven't been able to talk as you say, and this rain wasn't in my plans. It wasn't in my plans to end up in the apartment of a stranger at this hour when I should be at home. Sorry to say it, but I'm just reviewing the facts.- She was right; those were the facts, and viewed in that way, it didn't look very normal. Hence my concern for her friends who left her alone. I was about to interrupt her to ask about that when she continued, -The truth is, I should be at home packing. I have an early flight to catch tomorrow, and I can't stay here without finishing packing.- She paused for a bit too long for my taste; she was choosing her words carefully. -I need to leave, really.

I did not know what to say or think. I did not know whether to speak first and then think, so I decided on the former. I had just met the woman of my dreams, and now she had to pack and leave. Where to? For how long? When would she be back? So many questions. She had said the last sentence as if it was difficult for her. Did she not want to leave because she had met me? What was I thinking?

-Hey, calm down, okay? Let's talk about this while we get things sorted out here, and we'll figure out a way for you to get home in time, pack, and catch your flight. We have time,- I said. It was still raining very hard outside, and the thunderstorm was getting louder. The end wasn't in sight, and I wasn't sure if my words sounded convincing. - The first thing we need to do is dry your clothes and get you back to a normal temperature. I'm going to go down to the laundry room while you try to call a taxi service and plan for a pickup in an hour, and everything will be fine, okay?

She nodded and made a gesture of resignation. She looked back at me with gratitude and tenderness, and I once again felt the warmth of the heater, those looks were so pleasant, and I had grown accustomed to those sky-colored eyes looking at me with different messages. I took the bag of wet clothes, went to the drawer next to the closet where I keep the tokens for the washing machine, took some and a small bag of soap, just in case I had to wash and not just dry. I opened the door and looked at her before closing it. She had moist eyes and her head was a little low. She seemed saddened, but there was also a strange sparkle in her gaze.

I ran down the stairs thinking about how lucky I was to have met Carmela, and at the same time, the coincidence that I met her the day before I took a flight to who knows where. That meant that my opportunity to get to know her well was in the next few hours. On the other hand, experience had taught me that coincidencesdo notexist. So, what should I expect from all this? Who was Carmela and who was she going to be in my life?

The concert, the way we met, the seats together, the storm, the trip, everything was spinning and passing too fast in my head and in time. I arrived at the laundromat, took out the clothes from the bag, anddid not know what to choose, washing or drying or both. I thought that drying only took 45 minutes and both took 1 hour and 25 minutes, so I took the liberty of selecting the latter, more time.

As I took the clothes out of the bag, I realized that all of it, including the underwear, was in there. That meant that the beauty I left sitting on my bed with a giant sweater covering her arms and reaching halfway down her thighs had nothing underneath that sweater. I swallowed hard and stopped imagining things. My heart started beating rapidly, and blood rushed to my brain, so I was not thinking straight.

I took a deep breath and calmed down. I had to focus on the immediate and not the sublime. Everything I imagined and desired could become a reality only if I did things correctly and from sincerity and honesty. The coincidence of her being in that outfit in my studio did not give me any right to think or act improperly with her. I had never done it with any woman, and I was not going to do it now that I really liked Carmela. I left the machine in the laundromat to do its job and started to slowly climb the stairs. At each landing, I stopped to observe how the storm wasn't decreasing, and the lightning and thunder were becoming increasingly terrifying.

I do not remember how long it took me to climb the stairs, but it was much longer than usual. It was useful to calm down, and the thought of Carmela without underwear under my sweater was gone. It helped to remove all the cold that I could have had. I opened the door slowly, thinking about how to ask her about her trip and order all the questions without revealing the immense interest I had in her and how affected I felt for having met her just the night before my trip and in the conditions, we were in.

I found her sitting at the desk, looking at the storm through the window. The only light on was the one in the entryway between the bathroom and the bed area and the kitchen, so I could barely see her silhouette with one leg on the desk and the other almost touching the floor. Every time there was a lightning bolt, her face would light up and I could see her completely. She didn't feel my arrival due to the thunderous noise, so I could contemplate her tranquilly for a few seconds and through a few lightning bolts. She was completely absorbed with the view in the sky or whatever was visible in between the lightning storm and the rain. Her beauty combined with the natural fireworks display showed me a surreal image, drawn, and painted by the creators.

I approached slowly, and when I saw her thigh almost completely exposed due to the position she was sitting in, the thought I had in the laundry room came back, and I felt the heat again spreading through my body and landing in my lower abdomen. She lookedat me slowly, and I tried to hide my agitation, fortunately, the lights were off, and I looked a bit to the side, so Ido not think she figured out what was on my mind.

-I've already left everything working, your clothes will be ready in a while, and we can call a taxi so you can go home and pack,- I said, dragging out the last words with all the intention.

-Thank you very much, Miguel, you have been very kind, but I don't think it's going to be as simple as you say. I called several taxi services, and they are all suspended due to the storm. Most of them say that Newton is the most affected area, and it's not known when transportation will be restored,- she lowered her tone gradually as she gave me the news until her phrases almost didn't come out.

-I tried not to show alarm at what he said so as not to add tension to the moment - So we have nothing left but to get comfortable, talk and get to know each other better, don't you think? It's early and we'll be ready to go to your house and pack our bags at any time, I offer myself as the main baggage handler, I'm an expert at packing at the speed of light.

Of course, while I was talking, I was thanking heaven for this opportunity to have her a little longer in the studio and get to know her better, even the storm seemed pleasant to me, considering that rain is one of my favorite natural events.

-Yes, we have no choice,- she replied,nodding,and squinting her eyes in a very cute way and smiling about the suitcase.

-Well, let's start with the basics,- I said, -I have a bottle of magnificent Californian wine that I bought to drink all by myself when I got out of the concert, so we're in luck, we'll open it and catch up on each other's stories, how does that sound?

-Just you by yourself?- she asked.

-Sounds pathetic, doesn't it?

-Men, God.

-Don't believe me? Look at me, if you weren't here, I'd be very lonely.

-If the storm didn't come, you wouldn't be lonely at all,- she replied, making a face with her eyes and lips that made me want to bite her.

I loved that we were already playing word games and that kind of thing, I found the only two glasses I had, uncorked the bottle, and poured a normal amount so that there would be enough for at least three glasses each.

She was still sitting in the same position at the desk, I tried not to look at her leg so as not to lose focus on the conversation and show my agitation, I handed her the glass, cleared the rest of the desk for myself, and sat down in the same way in front of her.

-Okay, here we are then, now I want to know everything, where are you going? Why are you going? When are you coming back?

Everything. Cheers!- I said, we clinked glasses and took a sip. The wine was excellent, it was worth its price and fame.

She stared at me for a long time, which I appreciated given the beauty of her eye color and the tenderness of her gaze, I guessed she was trying to choose her words carefully again.

-I'm going home, it's a long, very long trip from Boston to Caxias do Sul,- she said very slowly and sadly.

With those words alone, I understood what she meant when she said it was a very long trip, she had probably done it several times in the years she had studied in Boston, but this one was very long because there was no return, it was going to be the last one, at least in her life as a student.-

I felt like someone had hit me in the head with a hammer, the apprehension that looking at her had caused me from the moment she told me she had to travel the next day, my race up the stairs and slow turn, all the indecipherable thoughts that had assaulted me during that time were now confirmed, I had only met her a couple of hours ago and the possibility of never seeing her again opened up like an unfathomable abyss. I saw her take a long sip of wine as if to dissolve the lump in her throat.

-God only knows how much I love this city,- she continued. -I grew up here. I came here very young five years ago. The first year was a lot of fun. I was just studying the language and I got to know every bar and club here. I also met my boyfriend, well, my ex,- she clarified at the expression I made. -It was a spectacular time. Then came the real university and things changed a bit. I had to study really, really hard. The first year was difficult, the opposite of the year I studied English.-

-I understand, I also love this city deeply, even though I haven't been here as long as you and I complain about the changing weather. But that's a minor thing compared to everything you grow as an individual here, both personally and culturally. The transfer of learning and experiences is immense.

-Yeah, I learned everything here, what life can teach you, how to get to know people, who your friends are and who aren't. Solitude teaches you things that you don't learn even if you get a million pieces of advice,- she continued in a very sad tone, like when you're giving a farewell speech.

-That place you're going to, is it your home? Have you always been there, are you going back to your parents?-

-Yes, yes, and yes,- she laughed. I felt like my questions were a bit obvious, but her sadness, like the one I was feeling, was capturing us and I wanted to rescue the moment. I returned her smile with a nod. -All your questions, yes. It's my home with my parents and siblings. But it's a village in the Brazilian Sierra Gaucha, completely unlike Boston. It's a place where grapes are grown to make wine.

-And does your family have vineyards?- I thought to myself that I was glad I had splurged on a good bottle of wine because I didn't want to imagine if I had bought a cheap one.

-Yes, we have vineyards, and we make wine, as good as this one we're drinking. Men make wine and women study medicine, except me, who went for an intermediate career, Biomedical Engineering.

-And are all the Brazilian women over there, I don't know how to pronounce it...

-Caixa do Sul.

-That, Caixa do Sul, are they like you?

-Like me? How? Explain.

-Beautiful, obviously,- I smiled. Why would you want me to tell you if you already know it?

-Yes, I think so. The Italian community is very large in that area. It's not like we're all the same, right? I mean, you can't expect that. But if you mean the typology, then yes,- her responses became more animated.

-And your last name is Italian?-

-Yes, Italian. Why?

-Well, to me it sounded very Portuguese, or Brazilian, I guess.

-Hahaha, it could be, but no. It's Italian.

Seeing her smile after having seen her so sad made me feel better. Hearing her talk slowly sometimes and excitedly others made my heart race. At the same time, when I looked inside myself, I felt a pain beginning to overwhelm me, a pain I had never felt before. It was like being in a dream of something wonderful happening to you. You know you're asleep and you don't want to wake up. You want to stay in the dream forever, but you know that when you wake up, you won't dream it anymore.

-And you, Miguel? I've told you everything about me, what about you?

-Hahaha, you haven't told me much, but let's accept that it was like an appetizer.-I paused. What did I want to tell her about myself? The truth was I wanted to tell her everything from the day I was born until the day I met her. That's not normal. I've never been the type of person to like talking about my life. I tried to organize my thoughts, but I was so focused on her, on every gesture, every word, that I didn't have a summary of myself prepared. -My life is very simple. I came to study Literature and Philosophy, and I'm a budding writer. I started writing very early. I began university in my hometown, but I got this opportunity to come to Boston with some friends who stayed for only a few months and left me here. I decided to continue with the greatest effort, but here I am. I may finish the degree this fall semester.

We continued talking, pouring ourselves a second glass of wine, telling each other about our childhoods, what we liked and did not like, the bad experiences with people who approach you in a country that is not yours, only with the intention of taking advantage of you.

I told her about the juggling I had to do to keep studying, how some months were tough, and others were very good, about the friends who came and went, and how sometimes I had to be a guide for those who had just arrived.

She explained that her boyfriend graduated a semester before her, went to Brazil, and she never heard from him again. No call, no message. That was a year ago, and she focused on studying so she could finish in the last fall semester. She stayed in Boston because she wanted to take two more electives, and she had finished them a week ago when the spring semester ended. That seemed part of the celestial conspiracy for this encounter. The boyfriend who disappeared, the electives, the concert, the seats together, the storm, her friends, her infinite blue eyes. I told her exactly that, and she stared at me.

-Do you realize that we're here talking like we've known each other all our lives? Do you know what time it is? Do you know that I have to take a flight to the other side of the world at 8:00 a.m.? Do you know that this storm may never end, and we may never see each other again?- The last sentence she trailed off very slowly, and something wet entered one of her eyes, magnified by the light of a lightning bolt that crossed the window.

-Don't worry about the time, Carmela. If there's something irrelevant in our lives, it's time. Humans live according to the clock and base everything on time. Neither you nor I know what can happen from the moment we step out onto the street and go to your house to pack our bags. Neither you nor I know if these hours we spend together can change our destiny, and neither you nor I know if this will just become a memory, and how many times we can relive it in our minds. What's important is the mark this moment leaves on our souls, our hearts, and our bodies.- It was close to midnight and the rain seemed to be easing up. We had talked enough and shared enough.

She stared at me intensely and a light shone from those two marine headlights, a light I had never seen before and that fascinated me, like a magnetic force emanating from those captivating eyes, pulling me in little by little. She lowered her gaze and suddenly I found myself submerged in the sweetest, softest lips I had ever kissed in my entire life. I felt the warmth I had experienced hours before, but this time it entered very slowly. It was no longer uncomfortable and sudden; it was a warm, pleasant temperature that flowed through my entire body. We did not touch, just the kiss, just our lips united in a slow but intense contact. With my eyes closed, I could perceive her smell, her taste, her sensations, her warmth. It seemed like an infinite moment, and I did not want it to end, and I could feel that she didn't want it to end either.

Very slowly we began to separate, she kept her gaze very low, I took her by the chin and looked directly into those bewitching eyes of hers, risking not knowing what to do or say, but I had to do it, I had to take the chance to see what I could find in her. She lowered and raised her eyelids and looked directly into my face, the message was very clear, she sighed heavily. Her eyes screamed at me, -Miguel, here I am, everything depends on you.

I lifted her off the desk where we had been sitting all this time, kissed her again but this time I pulled her towards me and hugged her, feeling her body, her endless curves, she pressed against me, and it was a complete fusion between us two, I could feel her legs around mine and her firm breasts against my chest. This time the kiss started very tenderly and continued to rise in passion and heat, it was much longer than the first one but not more tender or sweeter, this one had more of contained desire and explosion of repressed emotions.

I slowly withdrew, not stopping kissing her, not just on the lips, until I stopped her in front of me, took her by the shoulders and slowly lowered my hands to her waist and a little lower, grabbed the sweater by its lowest part and began to slide it up very gently without stopping looking into her eyes, she raised her arms when I reached shoulder height and I continued my task until the sweater was no longer on her, I threw it on the desk and stayed observing what was in front of me. Not even in my best dreams did I think I would find a living sculpture of such beauty. We looked at each other in the eyes and fell onto the bed next to us.

If I had understood any definition of making love before this night, from this moment on I changed it forever, time slipped between our skin without warning us that every touch, every breath, every touch would be tattooed in invisible and indelible ink, the pleasure of shared heat had no known earthly words to be described, I remember each of the kisses, each moan, and each gesture, one by one the looks and the closed eyes trying to sigh every drop of shared love that were engraved in my mind, although I didn't think, I just felt.

We fell asleep for a few minutes, I felt her move in the bed and woke up, she looked at me sleepily and whispered very quietly, -Now I want to know what time it is.- I looked for my phone and saw the time, it was 4:14 a.m., we got up, not without kissing each other again, I ran down the stairs again.

I picked up her clothes and ran back up, when I got there,she told me the taxi would be downstairs in the building in 10 minutes. If there was one good thing about this city, it was that it recovered from weather emergencies very quickly,I have seen 20 inches of snow fall and people continue with their lives as if nothing happened. I dressed quickly while not taking my eyes off her, with the light on she was much more beautiful and captivating.

-You don't really need clothes, you're much more beautiful naked,- I said. She smiled and continued dressing more slowly, I looked out the window walking backwards from where she was and she continued laughing. God, I loved that woman.

-Can I ask you a favor?- She asked me.

-What do you think?

- Yes or no, there's no time.

- You're back to talking about time, of course, yes.

- Sell me that suitcase you have in the closet, will you?

- Hahaha, why would I sell it to you? I'll give it to you, I'm dying to get rid of it - which was totally false because it was an important part of my closet, but just the thought of her taking something of mine made me feel great.

- Are you sure?

- Absolutely.

- It's just that at this hour, I won't have time to pack the rest of my things and organize them, and I have to act quickly because otherwise, we won't make it. By the way, you don't have to come with me to the airport and do everything you said you were going to do, it seems like too much work, don't you think? Besides, I'll be rushing against the clock and that doesn't seem to please you much.

- What I like is being with you and I'm going to enjoy it until the last minute - I replied - so I'll go with you, we'll pack your suitcase, and I'll take you to the airport. Well, not me, the taxi, which has already arrived. By the way, let's go down.

We went down slowly holding hands, looking at each other at every landing and giving each other a kiss. There were either too many or too few words, I do not know, but each station is a memory of her in this building. We got into the taxi, she gave the driver the address in Newton, and we sat very close to each other. She rested her head on my shoulder and seemed to fall asleep. I looked at her throughout the almost 30-minute ride, as well as the dark and semi-flooded streets of the city. On a curve that the driver took a little too fast, she woke up, looked at me, kissed me, and hugged me tighter, as if shedid notwant to let go. Idid notwant to let her go either, but Icould not show what I was feeling because that wasn't thememory, I wanted her to have of us.

We arrived at her friend's parents' house, where she was staying, as she had told me before. The rule was that I could notcome in because I was a friend, only her girlfriends could go up. But in this emergency moment, we had agreed that I would sneak in and help her pack her suitcase, and we would leave quietly.

That isexactly what we did, but it took longer than expected because she had a lot to pack, and the three suitcases were not enough. She had to choose what to take and what to leave behind, and she still had a lot of overweight. We had called the taxi a few minutes before and left the house with the sun rising at around 6:15 a.m., with just enough time to get to Logan Airport if wedid nothit much traffic.

During the time in her room, we only whispered and laughed at the mess and the way we packed the suitcases. I stole a couple of kisses, but as soon as we got in the taxi, the memory of the night assaulted us, and it was difficult to have a conversation without interrupting each other to kiss and caress. That served as a distraction for the heavy traffic we encountered, so we did not stress about the time. Without realizing it, we arrived at the airport. I got off quickly to take care of the suitcases, handed them to the valet who checks in the flight at the entrance outside, and she went with someone who took her ticket. She came back a few minutes later with the boarding pass in her hand. It was 7:01 am, she had 59 minutes left to go through immigration control and arrive on time for her flight.

She approached me slowly, stood in front of me, and did not say a single word. More than a minute passed, I did not want to interrupt her, time stood still for the two of us, we did not hear the noise of taxis arriving, or valet calling passengers, or buses parking behind us, we only existed, her and I, and the world had stopped, we were in the dimension of the infinite and enduring. She kissed me first on the cheek, then looked me in the eyes, she had already discovered what it caused in me, and she kissed me softly, tenderly, and slowly on the lips, without touching, without embracing.

I took her by the waist and hugged her, kissed her softly at first and then as if my life were ending in that very moment, a tear from her mixed with one of mine, it wasn't intentional, I had been holding back for a long time, I hadn't even realized that what I felt since I arrived at her house was that, the great desire to tell her don't go because if you go, I'm going to cry. She lowered her head and put a hand on my chest.

-I'm going to miss Boston, many things happened to me here, the best of my life I lived here, and the best because they taught me and made me the person I am today, not necessarily because everything that happened to me was good. Maybe I'll never come back, but you,

Miguel, are what I will remember most about this city, it's how you taught me, it doesn't matter how much time we spent together, what matters is how wonderful the moment we lived was,- she said, kissed me, turned around and ran towards the entrance.

I saw her running, she passed the door and mixed with the people towards the controls, I rushed after her, passed the entrance door, and stopped. I stood watching as she handed her boarding pass and passport to the airport security guards, turned towards where I was, and in the distance, I'm sure I saw her tears, and her eyes had a deep blue color like the ocean. It wasn't the same look from last night at the concert, light blue of innocence and life, it was darker as if she carried something in the depth of her heart that would accompany her forever.

I lost sight of her on one of the turns in the security line, I went back to the door, and went out to the street. The temperature had dropped since the storm, and I felt the cold air hitting my face, penetrating me to the bones, and why not say it, to the soul.

I decided to go back to the studio the long way, walked to the Blue Line station at Terminal A, took the train that would take me to Government Center station, and then took any Green Line car to get off at Park Street and walk again through the Boston Common.

It would take approximately an hour between trains, line transfers, and walking through the park. This time, I was not worried about the cold, only the pang of loneliness and nostalgia that I felt in my stomach. Memories started assaulting me: the moment she first looked at me at the concert, the run in the rain, when I opened the door and saw her sitting at the desk, when we kissed for the first time, when I lifted her sweater and her scent, her scent when we made love, everything came flooding back to mymind.

As I walked, I noticed that I had Carmela Costa's phone number registered on my phone, but it was the number she used in Boston. An alarm went off in me and the pain in my stomach increased. I quickly dialed her number, but it went straight to voicemail. As I reached the street level, I saw two missed calls from her and a message popped up: -"Adeus Miguel, espero que não me esqueça, não te esquecerei,"- it said. -Goodbye Miguel, I hope you don't forget me; I won't forget you.- She must have turned off her phone for takeoff, and there was no way to communicate with her.

Everything happened very quickly and time, well, time was not important. Only the moments I spent with her that were never erased from my memory.

THIRD STORY

I SEE YOU

Every now and then, we can allow ourselves to be a little old-fashioned, sometimes even a little cheesy sounding. It is not that we get too sugary, but when we want to say sweet things, it's not always appropriate to use our colloquial ways or language acquired from social media or daily slang. That is why I wrote this verse:

Let's be romantic,

leave each other a note,

steal a glance,

save a tear,

and give each other a smile.

*****

Normally, Alexander did not speak to Liza very often. She was always with her friends or coming down from her apartment surrounded by her brothers. It is not that he was intimidated by her brothers since they were his closest friends, but he tried not to get too close to her when they were around for fear of showing his discomfort. It would not be an easy task to explain to Ernesto, the oldest of the brothers, that he liked his little sister.

On the other hand, her friends were much more intimidating than Liza herself, not to mention her cousin Ronna, who looked like she came out of a fairy tale but dressed like a showgirl before entering the club.

That afternoon, they had all come down from the brothers' apartment with a cooler full of beers, and he was waiting for them downstairs. The group was complete. They started talking after greeting each other with the customary kisses, which he had to give to the girls since they all came together. Of course, he enjoyed each one, especially when Liza offered him her fresh, pink cheek that smelled of newly applied perfume. When the greetings were over, he watched the group and repeated what he had done hundreds of times, perhaps thousands, in the last year. I really like that girl! And it's so difficult for me to hide it.

-Hey, Alexander, what's wrong with you? Wake up, man,- he heard Oscar, Liza's youngest brother, reprimanding him while he was absorbed in watching her parade with her friends and cousin. -What are you thinking about? You're slow. Get the next round.- He meant that he had to take a beer for each one from the portable cooler they had hidden in the trunk of the car.

The meeting place was a wide hallway in the side exit of the building that led to the covered garage. There were several wooden benches on both sides before a low concrete fence that, at the back, had a garden with pink and white hibiscus. In the center of the garden squares, a coconut tree made the environment look very tropical. The sunset gave a glow to the plants that invited more to be hugged in pairs than to the bustle of several people all talking at the same time. However, this was not the case or the moment.

He counted them and there were nine in total: Liza, her three friends, her cousin, the three brothers and his own sister.

They had used his car to store the cooler, they were not sure if drinking alcohol outside the building was completely legal and did not want to expose themselves to any misunderstanding with the police while being in the area where they lived. He took out the beers and handed them out two or three at a time, saving the last one for Liza and making sure it was ice-cold. When he handed it to her, he held onto it for a second or two longer than normal. She looked up, met his gaze, and smiled. Suddenly, he let go of the beer, thinking it was going to fall to the ground, but she had been holding onto it for a while. Those amber-colored eyes with that perfect smile directed at him, along with a slight pout, were not exactly what he needed to calm the pounding in his chest when she was near.

He continued on his way, trying to hide the tremble he felt inside, but how could he know if it was noticeable or not when he felt his blood burning and his pulse racing? Fortunately, the group split into two, the men on one side and the women on the other. It was to be expected since Liza and her cousin, who was also the sister of the three brothers, were on the women's side, along with her friends, who, even though the brothers might think of them as three beautiful women, at least respected the presence of their sister in the group.

Oscar turned to him again, but this time the tone and perhaps more so the content of the question worried him.
-Alexander, I see you're very calm. You're not like that with women, and there are about five specimens here who are contesting for your attention, of course with the exception you already know. But what's going on with you, brother?

He was obviously referring to the fact that he was not even considering pursuing Liza, despite his reputation as a ladies' man. Imagine if that is what the younger brother thought, even though they were good friends, he was not of the same generation. How could he explain to Ernesto, the older brother, and his childhood friend, what he felt for his younger sister?

-No, man, what do you want me to do? We're not here to hit on anyone today, just to hang out and chat. Or did I miss something? What's the plan?

Normally, the group consisted of 15 or 20 young people, mostly from the same building or nearby buildings, but that day most of them had gone to other parties or were at home and did not come to the usual Friday gathering before heading out to a club or party later.

-There's no plan today, little brother,- Ernesto replied. -We're all hanging out here, so we might as well have fun with what we have. The three girl friends are serving the three of us well because they're not bad at all, and as usual, Liza's got some good stuff. And you're left out this time, because you can't go after her or Ronna. You don't mess with family, and besides, it's about time you left some for the rest of us, right?

Of course, everyone laughed at Ernesto's joke. These two had been best friends for many years, and the other two brothers knew about their escapades with both women and the parties they had that lasted for several days. But that had already begun to dissipate as the two of them advanced in their university studies.

In any case, Alexander thought, tonight he would just have to watch Liza from afar, as he had been doing for how long? Maybe for a couple of years? Since the girl had turned into a woman and suddenly showed off the most beautiful attributes he had seen in any other woman. The truth was that he had known her for a longtime but had never really paid attention to her as a woman. He always went to Ernesto's house, which was that Ernesto's house, never Liza's house.

And now, it wasn't even Ernesto's house anymore, and every day it was harder for him to visit his friend.

Time passed, and the two groups of men and women began to merge until they were immersed in a multiple conversation, where everyone was talking to everyone, making it difficult to communicate with words and follow the same conversation. Therefore, much of the conversation was through gestures and facial expressions, but at the same time, it was very fun, and the laughter and jokes between themdid not stop.

Suddenly, something unexpected happened. He never imagined that Liza would come closer and touch him, let alone lean a little on his arm. She put her head almost on his shoulder and whispered something that he could not hear well. The unease he felt being so close to her and her speaking almost in secrecy didn't allow him to understand what she had said. Now, he had a problem. He wanted to know what she had said, but itdid not seem right to pull her aside or ask her to repeat it in front of everyone.

She seemed to be waiting for a response from him and looked directly into his eyes with mischief and complicity, something he had never seen in her before, and which completely clouded his understanding. It was now or never.

-Sorry, honey, but I didn't quite understand you,- he tried to put on the best expression he could, while lowering his head and getting closer to her, hoping she would repeat what seemed to be a blatant flirtation.

-I said you're driving Ronna crazy. It's not possible that you haven't noticed,- she whispered in a very low voice, bringing her lips to his ear, which almost touched. -Everyone says you're a womanizer, but in this case, you haven't even noticed her a little bit, so here I am doing a little favor,- she laughed at the end of the sentence.

Unintentionally, his gaze immediately went to Ronna's eyes, who returned the gaze with a sensual smile and gesture. As he turned his head back to Liza, he realized he had made a big mistake. She nodded her head as if to say, -There you go, I've finished my job.- The last thing he wanted was for Liza to step away, thinking that the next step was for him to approach Ronna and consummate whatever that goddess had planned for him.

-Think fast,- he told himself, unsure why it was so hard for him to react quickly in the presence of this girl, despite being so skilled with women. She wasn't much younger than him, but she was the younger sister of his friends, for God's sake. He had been with girls his own age or older, even married women, at the university recently, but in front of her, he felt slow and awkward.

-Wait, don't go. Explain this to me,- he managed to say, trying to hold her back and repair the damage done with the eye contact with Ronna.

-There's nothing to explain, it's very clear. Didn't you see it with your own eyes?- Her tone changed to reproach, and the pout on her face shifted.

What exactly did she see in his face? Was she reproaching him for what he knew he had done with Ronna, the look of acceptance, the crossing of intentions? Wasn't that what she wanted? What was happening?

-Wait, wait, wait, now I don't want you to move an inch from this arm,- he said, regaining his confidence. There was something in the air that could be touched and cut, and he looked at her intently, as if trying to dominate and hold her. -You come here to tell me that Ronna wants something with me, and you don't say anything else?

He was trying to forget the eye contact, of course. He hoped it would work.

-Ha ha, look at the innocent baby, I hinted at something, and now you can see it for yourself. Now you're going to blame me because-- There was no doubt in her tone this time; she spoke with a lot of resentment and a little bit of anger.-No, you take responsibility and go over there. She's waiting for you.

He never would have imagined that Liza would express herself in that way, with such a deep feeling at the surface. The connection in their gaze was profound, gentle, immense. He stayed for a moment in those honey-amber eyes, bathing in their aura and enjoying their magnetism. He forgot about the world around him, and the voices of the group were distant and muffled. Only this pair of eyes that devoured and consumed him existed in this moment.

They looked at each other for so long, or maybe it was only an instant. He began to see how her lower lip trembled, and this filled him with the tenderness he felt when he used to watch her from afar. Now that he had her so close, that tenderness rose and covered all his senses. Where were all these feelings of both of them hidden, that they had not connected before? He wanted to stay in that gaze forever.

-Liza! Be careful, don't get too close to him,- Pablo shouted from the other side, the second of her brothers. -You know his reputation precedes him.- Everyone burst out laughing and continued their conversation without paying much attention to the two of them, but Pablo's call cut the moment of ecstasy.

-Well, I'll continue on my way, if you'll excuse me,- Liza continued. -I don't want you to think I'm the one interested here.

-No way, you can't go,- he said firmly. Pablo's call had helped them regain their composure, and now she looked very different from the moment of connection they had shared. But he knew the connection was there, it existed, and it was real.

-And why not?

-For several reasons, first of all, you can't come here and tell me to look over there where someone is waiting for you as if I was that easy,- he tried to lighten the tension with a joke. She smiled. -Second, what makes you think I want to leave with Ronna? And third, I'd rather stay here and talk to you.- He didn't even plan to use that last reason, but the sincerity with which he said it surprised even himself, and although it came out on its own without thinking, he didn't regret it one bit. It seemed the beers were doing their job.

-Well, that is a surprise,- she said, ignoring the first two reasons. -I thought the youngest of the brothers meant nothing to you. Since when you prefer to stay and talk to me?- She sounded quite sincere as well.

His chest tightened with reproach. She was right, he had been trying to ignore her for a long time and barely greeted her, a mandatory kiss and then no eye contact, just a sideways glance to appreciate every part of her that drove him crazy. That was the only way to keep going to that house without disturbing the peace of the friendship with her brothers. So Liza had been just a shadow for a long time.

From this moment on, hedid not have time to think. Every word he said came from the deepest part of his heart. He had been holding them back for the last two years, and they did not come out in the order they were supposed to, as he never made the slightest attempt to organize them. He had always thought they would never come out.

-It's not a surprise, Liza. You know very well that I have been watching you, paying attention to you,- he said. And suddenly, time and space were suspended in a vapor, taking the couple away from the surrounding noise. The words were not sound coming from his voice; they seemed more like a deep silence of sublime communication between two hearts, two souls, a man and a woman destined to look at each other in the past, present, and future.

Alexander continued as if his age and youth had changed to the most romantic of ancient troubadours, -Falling in love with you every day, trying not to get lost in your honey-colored eyes, trying to disguise what was growing inside me. And while I avoided you, the more dependent I became of seeing you again, that's why I visited your brothers every day, no matter which of them was in your apartment. I just needed to be close to you, even if I couldn't talk to you, touch you, or kiss you, as I so often desired. The surprise is rather that I have been able to contain myself all this time. But now you know, I've finally been able to tell you, so don't ask me to look at anyone else.-

Liza stood still, not knowing what to say or how to react. Several seconds passed, which felt like an eternity for both. He looked at her softly and tenderly as he had never been able to before, relieved, without the burden of all the time he had to keep quiet, with the satisfaction of being able to honestly look from the heart at the person he liked beyond his understanding. She was stunned by what she had just heard. She felt every word he said on her skin, like a caress, like the delicate breeze that brushes and refreshes. She tried to enjoy them syllable by syllable, what she had always dreamed of what she had always thought were her fantasies.

Alexander, the best friend of her older brother, the one she could never see as a man but rather as another brother, had told her everything she wanted to hear from a man her age. The seconds passed and they continued looking at each other in the same way since Alexander stopped talking. She knew she had to give a response, say something, react in some way. She did not want this moment to end and for him to forget what he said. Suddenly, she realized that if she did not react, these words would disappear, and everything would return to how it was before - cold, distant, like two strangers who only exchanged occasional glances that only they understood. Then her amber eyes opened in astonishment and desperation.

Alexander saw her eyes and didn't understand. At first, he thought there was a connection, but then her eyes opened wide, and he thought he saw a chasm that separated them. He then only managed to say, -I'm sorry, Liza, but if you...

She interrupted him, this time touching his lips with her index finger very softly, -I don't kiss you here because my brothers are around. You have no idea how long I've been waiting for this, or how much time I've spent wishing to hear everything you just said.- She was surprised by her audacity, by what she had just said, but she didn't regret it. It was worse to let it pass, to let him go, to feel that fear from a moment ago when she thought she might regret it.

When she touched his lips and squinted to tell him what she had just heard, Alexander felt that the ground beneath him disappeared, and he understood that the step he had just taken was the right one. This was the woman he had been waiting for, the one he would probably fall in love with forever.

-I'll have time to kiss you as much as you want. I assure you that your desire is less than mine,- he said. She blushed and looked at him again with sweet and caressing eyes.-That's more than I can handle right now,- she said.

-And what do you want me to do? Looking at you is the only thing I have right now. We can't even escape because we're under strict military surveillance, hahaha,- he smiled and bit his lower lip, no longer sounding nervous or distressed.

-I know,- she replied, adoring that gesture, and continued, -you know, a little while ago, I sounded a bit old-fashioned, romantic, almost cheesy, right?- She began to apologize for her old-fashioned declaration.

-But I've never been like that, youknow. Those were the words that came out of me at that moment, I don't even know where they came from...

-You know what? Those are the most beautiful words anyone has ever said to me in my short life, and I'll always remember them. I'll carry them with me forever,- she said.

-Wow, now it's you, that's great. We're both being a bit romantic and old-fashioned, aren't we?- he joked.

-Touché, my friend, touché. Hahaha, you made me wait a long time.

- Hey, you two there - a shout was heard from the other side of the group - it was Oscar, the youngest of the brothers, who approached - what's going on here, why are you plotting something without telling everyone?

Then, in a very low voice just for the two of them, he said - Look Liza, all you had to do was get this guy to talk to our cousin, nothing more, right? Or is there something else?

- Well, no - she replied - nothing more, just that this gentleman doesn't want to be convinced because it seems he doesn't like Ronna very much.

- Oh my God, brother, you're crazy. I don't like getting involved with family, and Ronna... well, I won't say anything, but this doesn't seem like you. They're practically handing her to you on a silver platter...

- It's not that, she doesn't know what she's talking about. It's just that she's your family, and I don't know, I never looked at her that way.

Liza looked at him as if to indicate that he had made a mistake by using the family excuse, and he returned the gaze with a smile that said, -I was about to tell her everything.- They smiled and the three of them separated. Each one returned to the initial group, she with her cousin and friends who didn't take their eyes off her for a second while she was talking to Alexander, and who of course wanted a detailed description of what they talked about, and he went with his friends, her three brothers, to continue talking about cars, women, and football.

She told her friends anything and nothing at the same time, she made up stories, but she never admitted or revealed what really happened between the two of them. She entertained them with lies and jokes, and the Ronna issue was settled with -My dear, you'll have to wait or do something extraordinary for that man to notice you. Anyway, I don't think so, because he seems to really like someone else.- There would be time to tell her that the other person was herself, and time would take care of putting things in their place. After all, Ronna was just a whim, but what she felt was something else, right?

Alexander, on the other hand, stayed talking with his friends, and the rest of the night went by with the certainty that every time he turned his gaze towards the group of women, he would find those deep honey-colored eyes correspond to his intentions, his secrets, his desires, and why not say it: his love.

FOURTH STORY

I CAN FEEL YOU

Extrasensory perception has been investigated for at least the last 200 years. All kinds of experiments, tests, and verifications have been proposed, but for one reason or another, which can range from falsification of evidence by those involved, greatly damaging this field, to a lack of scientific rigor or sabotage by researchers, today it is considered a pseudoscience and is given very little attention in serious scientific circles.

Extrasensory perception has entered other more eclectic fields and we see it as part of all kinds of spiritual movements. Humanity has taken for granted, without proof as mentioned above, that the ability of clairvoyance or remote viewing, precognition or retrocognition is an intrinsic part of each person, in some more developed than in others, and there are even courses and programs for everyone to learn and develop these skills.

Of course, as someone who enjoys all these topics, I have not been able to stay away from researching and searching for these phenomena, for their verification, which although not scientific, is at least in the form of anecdotes and shared experiences.

Another aspect that has always caught my attention is when two people share a very deep feeling, such as a mother and child, twin siblings, close friends, or lovers. These people often say to each other -I woke up thinking about you and you called me- or the startled mother who calls her child who is in another city or country and says, -I do not know, I felt something and I'm calling to see if you're okay. These are familiar phrases, almost daily among us, which we say in a very normal way without stopping to think about the spiritual depth that this entails.

Meditating specifically on lovers, people who are in love or who were, who have just come together or who have ended a great love, but it could not be, is what led me to write this verse:

How is it that I feel
your thoughts connected to mine every time,
how is it that your gaze makes me dream
about what you experience within.

* * * * *

I will never forget the date of June 10th. That day I entered the Ariztimuño & Fermonsel Law Firm for the first time. It was the interview with the Human Resources department. They subjected me to all kinds of tests, knowledge, and legal issues that I had never heard of in my short experience and at the university. They gave me a psychometric test in which I had to draw, and I, who am best at drawing a stick figure with a round head that looks like an alien, a test of English that I did not understand the point of. If we struggle to write legal topics in Spanish, how could they expect us, the new ones, to write in another language? They sent me to the doctor for a pre-employment test, gave me a free topic to write my opinion on, and I think that was the onel did the best on. I wrote everything that came to mind, and two days later they called me back to say that I could work for them at the firm.

Then on June 17th, I had the formal interview with the boss, Jose Ariztimuño. I did not know who he was and had never seen a picture of him, but his name was on the firm, so he was definitely important and probably had a lot of money.

I had graduated from law school two months earlier, and during that same time, I had been looking for a job in all kinds of companies and law firms. I wanted to work in something related to what I had studied. Idid not want to waste the effort of five years in college, with all the help my parents gave me to finish the degree. The least I could do was to develop as a lawyer.

I was losing patience and was about to give up. I had gone to several interviews and had plastered the city with my resume when a friend told me that this firm was looking for recent graduates to train them as international lawyers. She suggested that I apply. I was about to ignore her advice since what did I know about international law? But suddenly, a gut feeling decided for me, and I filled out the application she had given me.

I applied in person to the job, I went to the office, it was an immense building in the financial area of the city, the offices were impressive, all made of black Marquina and white Carrara marble, I could not even believe I could work there. But my hunches had taken me far on other occasions, and I wanted to see where this one would take me.

When they called me for the exams, I got very excited and thought that at least the hunch had served to have one of the few opportunities to take an exam and go to an interview in the last two months.

When the exams were over, the hunch had disappeared and, in its place, I felt a great desolation, all those exams and tests were for experienced lawyers, for people with deep knowledge of complex legal issues and on top of that in English, it's not that I didn't know anything about the language, but God, drafting is another thing. How could I even imagine that I could work in a place like that? I graduated with very good grades and made friends with several professors who appreciated me a lot, but this type of job was for the children of friends of the owners, for those who went to theclub and played golf with the main partners of the law firm, how could I even imagine that they would pay attention to a newly graduated lawyer who has never worked before? That was as far as my hunch had taken me, as I called them.

But the dream continued, they called me and gave me a date, June 17th at 8:00 a.m. with the main boss. When I received the call, I did not let the girlon the other sidefinish or even ask her name, I let out a scream that made her burst out laughing on the other end of the phone, I couldn't stop jumping and shouting. She had the patience to wait for me to calm down to give me clear instructions. According to her, I had to arrive on time, that is, a few minutes before 8 since the boss was very strict and the interview would start at the exact time.

He also gave me the dress code, nothing less than a complete suit preferably in a dark color. -Pleasedo not arrive late or with a brown jacket,- she clarified with a sweet voice, still laughing. Ultimately, my premonition came true, and I would be working at one of the best, most prestigious, and exclusive law firms in the country.

The following two days, I celebrated with my friends, drinking all the beers Ihad nothad in the two months I was job hunting. Whenever I had a moment of clarity, I would worry about the suit, shirt, shoes, and tie, but I would just grab another beer and forget about it.

On Saturday, I woke up with a severe headache. I was not sure if it was from drinking too much or from worrying about the jacket and its accessories. I had 48 hours to solve the problem. I thought about my graduation suit, but I had made the mistake of buying a light blue one because it was trendy, and I liked it. I did not have any alternatives but to borrow money from my dad to buy a new suit and hopefully some shoes too because the ones I had worn to graduation were old and not up to par.

In fact, my dad could only lend me money for a modest suit. Itwas not the best cut or fabric, but at least it met the requirement of being dark. My father was worried because hedid not know if I was being hired as a lawyer or a funeral agent, but I explained that it was normal because prestigious lawyers make a lot of money burying their opponents' hopes and sometimes their clients' too. He was interested in the "a lot of money" part and stopped making fun of me for the rest of the weekend.

He had made a great effort to lend me the money, and we were not doing well financially, but I was confident that I could be successful in that job and soon repay him for the suit and all the support he had given me throughout my education. It was my most cherished dream. I had not even started working, and I was already in debt.

The much-anticipated day, June 17th, arrived, and I was already at the law firm's door on the 42nd floor at 7:45 a.m. The Ariztimuño & Fermonsel offices started on the 39th floor, and this floor was closed. No one had arrived yet. I stood staring at the name and did not realize that a figure had walked past me and opened the door. It was 7:50 a.m. I remember it every time I get to this floor.

She opened the door and turned around. I had never seen anything like her before. I had never been standing face to face with such a beautiful woman. She looked like a ceramic doll sculpted by the gods. She had a white skirt that fit tightly at the hips and legs, a turquoise blouse, and a dark blazer that made her matte white skin stand out, making any color she wore look outstanding.

-You must be Adrian...- she said to me.

-Urriaga, Adrian Urriaga at your service, and your name is?- - it was the same person who called me on the phone to give me the news that I had been accepted and who made the appointment with Mr. Ariztimuno.

-Sorry, I am Doctor Ariztimuno's assistant and my name is Jimena Llovera.- - luckily, I have never been shy or lazy to talk to women, because she took my breath away and her body, her walk, and her face could intimidate any other man, but not me, no way- -your surname is very uncommon, isn't it?- - she continued with her sweet voice and a tone of more confidence than when we first introduced ourselves.

-Well, yours is not one that you find in the neighborhood either, right?- - the fresh and clear smile from the phone call emerged, but if I was already caught off guard when I first heard her over the phone, this time seeing her lips was like poetry written on a honey spring. We entered and continued walking towards the offices.

-No need to address me formally, are we, the same age?

-Well, that depends, are you still 21? Yes. - she continued laughing. I think I could spend the whole day and all the months making her smile and be spellbound looking at her.

-I don't think you're 21.- we had already arrived at her desk, she pointed to a sofa in a small room next to her cubicle and suddenly became very serious, took a leather folder that had a notebook and entered the office that had a dark mahogany door with an impressive golden handle.

Seeing her and talking to Jimena made me forget why I was on this floor, I realized that I had not prepared any speech, I did not know what the interview was about, and I did not know if the gentleman or

Doctor, as she called him, had already arrived and what she had gone to do inside. She came out and signaled me that I could go in. He was there, apparently.

-Like this? Without anesthesia or anything?- I passed her by and whispered. I entered and out of the corner of my eye, I saw her smiling.

-Good morning, Lawyer Urriaga, please sit down, my name is Jose Ariztimuno.- he was a man in his fifties, with a perfectly trimmed beard that was starting to whiten in some parts, with small and intelligent eyes and a penetrating gaze, tall, but not too much. He was standing and offered me his hand across the desk.

What impressed me was his suit, I could not help it and I felt dressed like a clown, the dark gray cashmere fabric and the perfect cut with a white shirt with cuffs tied with gold cufflinks and the also dark tie that fell perfectly to the belt, made me turn to look at my shoes and discover the stains that the polish couldn't erase. I felt embarrassed and did not know what to do, I think he noticed it because he made an additional signal for me to sit down, without inspecting my clothing like I did with his.

-Thank you very much, Doctor Ariztimuño, and thank you also for considering me for the position in your law firm.

-Well, don't thank me so much, but let's start from the beginning. You don't need to call me Doctor. I imagine you heard it from my assistant. Here, we don't address each other as Doctor, lawyer, or anything like that. We call each other by name. So, from now on, you can call me José, and I will call you Adrián, if that's okay with you. - I nodded my head. - Okay, I was saying that you don't need to thank me so much. If you were hired, it wasn't because of my decision, which had nothing to do with it, but rather because of the results of your exams, your grades in university, and a few recommendations we received. - I was surprised by everything he said, from the first word to the last. If I was confused by his attire, I was even more so by how the conversation had started.

-Thank you very much. Well, excuse me, you told me not to thank you, but I don't understand very well. What recommendations are you referring to? - This part was the only thing I could admit in front of him. But the tests? Had I done well on the tests?

-As you can see, we are one of the most important law firms in the country, and you wouldn't think that we take things lightly. With time, you will realize for yourself that we don't. We handle all kinds of cases, and we evaluate the people we hire very carefully. We have various types of evaluation, and you already went through the written and medical tests. Before we even called you for those tests, we conduct a background check on the person that covers everything, including criminal, judicial, academic, and personal records. During the academic check, we found out that some of my friends from law school were your professors like International and Maritime Law, and those professors personally spoke to me about you. Their references were not only very good, but also interesting, especially because in all the years that I have known them, they had never spoken about a student in theway that they did about you.

-Wow, José, I really don't have words to... - I didn't have words. Thankfully, he interrupted me, because I didn't know what to say. I was so shocked that I felt dizzy and disoriented. I knew the professors. I had even developed a certain friendship with them. One of them had taught me more than one course. But for them to call the law firm and give recommendations about me was something Icould nothave imagined. And how did they find out that I was participating in this job offer?

-You don't need to have words, as I said, it's our job to make sure that the people who enter our law firm, besides being academically prepared, are the right people to have a long and fruitful career with us. And I mean -right- in every sense of the word, mentally, ethically, and personally. Do you have any questions about this?

-I have many questions, maybe too many. There are so many going through my head that I can't organize them. - He looked at me expectantly, as if he were waiting for me to ask at least one question. So, I asked the first one that came to mind. - How much and what part of the personal aspect do you investigate?- I did not understand this part. What did they know about me personally?

-Well, everything we can investigate, as I told you, we are a very powerful law firm and when you fill out the job application form, there are some small letters in which you give us permission to investigate everything about you that we want. Did you read them?- I nodded, but to be honest, I thought they were just dead letters. -We don't put those small letters there as decoration, we use them, and we have an investigation department that does its job, so they find out, because that's the right word, everything about you, your parents, your family, your close friends, your hobbies, in short, everything. Let me see what it says here, I know your father is a truck driver for a food transportation company, that your mother is a primary school teacher, and that your sister is a teenager and still studying in high school.

Anyway, a good family,- he continued. I had never felt so violated in my privacy before, this man was reading a summary of my life and concluding that we were a good family, as we really were, but not with such ease. Becoming a good family had cost us a lot, both my parents and me and my sister, resisting the attacks of poverty and not taking the path of vices like many others, it was a very tough battle day by day in our neighborhood. He looked at me and I could not figure out how to respond, so I lowered my gaze.

-Look Adrian, I know it's hard to sit there and listen to everything I'm telling you, but we are professionals and today you are entering the corporate world of the profession, you'll get used to this. Besides, there's nothing to be ashamed of in your investigation, on the contrary, you should feel very proud of your family, yourself, and everything you've done to be in this interview today. We evaluated 102 candidates and of those, you and 11 other lawyers are entering the firm with you. They are down there waiting for the introductory course, and you are here with me right now because I asked to welcome you specially. You know why?- I shook my head. -Because of all this background I have here on my desk, evidence of your ability and potential. We rarely recruit someone like you, and I wanted to be the one to welcome you.- He had read in me everything that I had not been able to express in the interview.

-I'm sorry, Jose, but everything you said took me by surprise and made me remember all the difficulties we went through at home to have a decent meal three times a day and to be able to study. If I graduated a little later than the others, it was for the same reason. At some point when my dad lost his job, I had to drop out to help with the household expenses, and to be honest, with all the weight of my soul, I went back to university because it hurt me to leave my dad with the burden of expenses and my studies. I also did odd jobs when I could.

-We are aware of that here, Adrian, and that is precisely what we have valued. Your professors and I have had a long conversation, and they have been able to tell me several things that I like about the way you have faced adversity.

-I thought I didn't have a chance with you guys, that you only hired daddy's kids who were your friends,- I blurted out without thinking. As soon as I finished speaking, I felt like I had made a mistake. I had managed to steer the interview in the right direction, but I had ruined it.

Dr. Ariztimuño burst into a very loud laugh, and that finally broke the ice in the conversation.

-You're absolutely right,- he said to me, -that's what we normally do, that's what all the big law firms in this country usually do -- and he continued laughing,-- and your statement confirms that I was right about you - The thing is, we don't get many people like you. Down there, you'll be with about nine 'daddy's boys or girls' and a couple of good students recommended by big firms or partners of this same firm. What I want is for you to come down and during the next two weeks of the introductory course, show why you're here, without being the son of a famous lawyer in the city or having recommendations from another firm. You're here because you deserve it, for your knowledge and your eagerness to learn. That's all you have to do.

-And you're telling me I have nothing to thank you for? Listening to you talk, it seems like my entry here is your bet against someone else. Do I have a detractor to watch out for? If so, tell me who so I know who to watch my back from.

-Sharper than I thought, Adrian. Never lose that quality and never be afraid to speak up, no matter who you're with. No, you don't have any detractors. And yes, it is my bet. The only detractor you'll have here is yourself, when you don't value yourself enough and don't believe you can achieve it. That's the basis of everything, you have to believe it. And do you want to know why you're my bet?

-Of course, I want to know,- I said enthusiastically.

-Because 29 years ago, many more than you have now, I was the one sitting in that chair, behind this desk, not exactly that chair or this desk, but a similar one in another building in a law firm that didn't have my name. Today, after all those years, the first name of the law firm is mine and I'm the managing partner and the one who makes the most money. I come from where you come from, I grew up with a story similar to yours, I did the same thing as you, I had parents with shortcomings like yours and I believed in myself, I believed I could reach the top. I entered a law firm full of 'daddy's boys' and worked very hard and did it with a lot of sacrifice. I lost a lot of things along the way, things that aren't noticeable today, but that I remember every morning when I wake up.

-Thank you very much, and don't tell me I have nothing to thank you for because I will do everything in my power to not disappoint you, so that you don't have a single complaint about my behavior and so that someday the law firm will be called Ariztimuño Fermonsel & Urriaga, or who knows, maybe Urriaga will come first and the money will stay here in this pocket you see.

Jose almost fell out of his chair, I think his suit got wrinkled from the sudden movement, but of course he returned to his initial state. That kind of quality does not disappear just like that.

-What I will tell you,- he said between laughs, -is that you have a mishmash of how to address me, mixing 'tu' with 'usted' and 'Jose' with 'usted' and vice versa. Save the formal address for when we're with clients, in court, or in a trial. While we're in the law firm, we're Jose and Adrian.

-Ok, I'll try, I promise.

-Again?

We both laughed at the same time.

-Now, when we finish here, you will ask my assistant Jimena for your contract, sign it, and take it to Human Resources. Then you go straight to the floor where the course is being given. Don't be late, the first day is very important, and I know the instructors, they are very strict.

He stood up and shook my hand. The interview was over, and we said goodbye. I promised that everything would go well, and he offered his support whenever I needed it, telling me never to leave without talking to him first. He told me that the other partner had founded the law firm almost 100 years ago and those two partners were the founder's grandchildren. They did not have the surname, so there was a chance that the law firm would be called Ariztimuño & Urriaga. It was the last game of the day, and I left the office.

As I walked through the door, I returned to reality. I had never experienced anything so surreal. I came to an interview where I did not know what to say or what to expect from one of the most prestigious lawyers in the country, and this person praised me and raised my self-esteem. I did not understand anything, but the reality I was returning to interested me much more. When I left, I saw Jimena in front of me. She got up from her seat and approached me, interested in how the interview went.

-How was the interview? -the question surprised me.

-There's a conspiracy here, like I'm the son of an Arab sheikh, and I don't know it, and you guys do, or I'm the heir to some fortune. First the doctor, as you call him, and now you're interested. -with her, I was determined to use direct ways of speaking, no -you- or -ma'am,- she didn't look like it.

-It's okay if you don't want me to ask or don't want to tell me, no problem. -she said with a sweet voice, a funny gesture, and an amiable tone, but laughing in a way that made me want to talk to her all day.

-No, if it were up to me, I'd tell you word for word, one after the other, so we can be here until 6 pm. But I have to go to Human Resources, sign the contract, and then go to the course to meet the colleagues, the teachers, etc. As you can see, I'm a very busy lawyer, but I can make time in my schedule, and we can have lunch. How about that? Then, when we see each other, we can tell each other everything. -I loved making her laugh.

-I don't have freckles, and I don't have lunch around here, so it's hard for that busy lawyer to fill that space in his schedule. Besides, you can't go to Human Resources if I don't give you the contract to sign, and I sign as a witness. -I said all that, drowning in laughter and shaking my head from side to side, making her long blond hair travel from one shoulder to the other. I had never seen such a charming gesture in a woman in my 25 years of life.

-Well, let's sign it because that's what we're going to live on, and it depends on the future of our children. -I went all out.

The laughter was so long and loud that I was afraid that Doctor Ariztimuño would come out and scold us for making a scene at work. She understood my panic.

-Don't worry, hecan't hear anything there.- she continued laughing - So, our lives depend on this? Then sign it quickly and try to get promoted faster so our kids can have a good future. Was I playing along? Or was I imagining things too quickly?

She handed me the contract in a sealed envelope. I read it slowly, afraid it might have the small print that I told Jose I had read in the interview but never saw. I moved away and sat on the sofa where I had waited to be called into the Partner's office.

Thank goodness I was sitting down when I saw the salary, they were offering me, which I supposedly had to accept. It was three times what a newly hired lawyer would make in a normal law firm. I knew this because several friends had already found jobs in other law firms, and what they would pay me in the first year of the contract, as it said there, was three times the average paid in other places. It was also about four times my parents' combined salary. My legs were shaking, and I did not know whether to cry or scream with joy in that very room. Jimena said that Jose could not hear me, so it was very possible that I could shout.

- Is everything okay, Adrian? Is there something wrong with the contract? Do you have any doubts? We can call Human Resources. - Jimena was very close. I did not know whether to look up or if my eyes were teary or showed complete discomfort. I gradually looked up, and her body looked sculptural from bottom to top. I could embrace her from the legs and waist and not let go, but her sweet and compassionate voice reached me very deeply, and my voice broke.

- No, nothing is wrong. It's just that seeing the contract, I don't think we have to wait any longer, Jimena. We can get married right away. - This exit was perfect because we both burst out laughing, and I regained my composure. I stood up suddenly so as not to be in a disadvantaged position and almost hugged her for real. She was not scared and withdrew slowly, allowing me to smell her perfume, and then the dizziness passed, from the money vertigo to the woman who was taking my breath away.

- No, really, no one like you has appeared around here, Adrian. You'll have to be careful because if you make those same jokes with other administrative staff or lawyers, you'll end up married in a month.

- No, Miss Llovera, the only person I would marry, not in a month, but in a week, is you. So don't dodge the question. It's all yours. - She continued to laugh. - Do you have a pen to sign?

- Yes, of course. Sign it because everything depends on it. But are you going to tell me what was bothering you on the couch? You looked sad.

-It's very simple, I don't know where you come from or your story, but if we're going to get married, I have to be honest with you from the beginning.- She looked at me with a mocking expression, and I became serious. -My family doesn't have the resources that you must be accustomed to seeing in this environment, like those of Doctor Ariztimuño and the other partners, or the lawyers who come from wealthy families and whose parents send them here to learn and then return to their companies or law firms. We are humble in social position. Look at me, this suit that I thought would suffice is new and looks like rags compared to the clothes that everyone else is wearing that I've seen today, and I can't imagine when I go down to class and see the other 11 classmates that I'll have to deal with from now on. I'm not saying that they think poorly of me; I'm not going to judge them because I'm not like that and I don't share that attitude of prejudice, but these are facts. I can't change them, and I have to accept them as they are. Then this contract comes along and offers me the salary of my father and mother combined for four months. It was all very shocking to me.

-But if you have achieved something like this Adrian, it's because you deserve it, it's because God had it destined for you, because your efforts have been rewarded by Divinity and have not been in vain, and everything you have lived has taught you and prepared you to face your future with humility and gratitude. - her words left me astonished, I never expected to hear such affirmations from a woman of 21 or 22 years old, she seemed more like a litany from my mother or grandmother, who was this woman?

-Young lady, are you the Virgin Mary herself?

-Don't you take anything seriously?

-It's not that, on the contrary, what I told you I said from the heart, and I was surprised that a woman your age, how many?

-Twenty-two.

-At 22 has so much understanding and beauty in her heart, women at your age are morefrivolous, aren't they? Or am I wrong?

-I don't know if they're more frivolous, but you told me that you didn't know my story and right now, but it will be another opportunity when I have time to tell you because they're calling me from there - and she pointed to the dark mahogany door - and I have to go, goodbye Adrian, I hope everything goes well and welcome - she took the leather folder and disappeared through Jose Ariztimuno's officedoor.

I stayed a couple of minutes more, I still had time, it was 20 minutes to 9, I just had to go and leave the contract in Human Resources and then go one floor down where the course was going to be taught. I wanted to calm my emotions, it had all been very intense, the interview, Jose, Jimena, the contract, the perspective of the future, in the morning when I woke up I didn't imagine I was going to have so many impacts together and it had been less than 60 minutes since I walked into the Law Firm. I looked at the closed mahogany door, I pictured Jimena talking to Jose, were they commenting on me? Hard to know.

As I stood in front of the elevator, I felt again that I was in Jose's office, I could see Jimena sitting in the same chair that I used, she was taking notes and looking at the notebook inside the folder, I sensed her heart beating fast under the turquoise blouse, suddenly she startled and I turned as if I had been pushed, the elevator doors had opened and there were several people inside.

I took the elevator, went down to the floor where Human Resources was, I asked who I could deliver the contract to and they pointed me to a door, I knocked and there were two young people sitting signing their contract too, the older woman on the other side of the desk smiled at me and extended her hand for me to hand her the envelope I had.

-Did you read it well? You must be Adrian Urriaga, right?

-Yes, I read it well and yes, I'm Adrian too.

-Ok, Adrián, that's all. One more thing, did you sign it in front of a witness? It can't be someone from Human Resources.

-Yes, I signed it in front of Jimena Llovera, the assistant...

-Yes, I know who she is. Did she also sign as a witness?

-Yes, everything is there.

-Perfect, then thank you very much. My name is Rosalía Fernández, and I am at your service for whatever you need. Anyway, in the course, you will have a module on Human Resources, and you will learn everything you need to know about the department's operation. Now it's good for you to go down; you don't want to be late for the course.

-Thank you, Mrs. Rosalía. -I left and took the elevator to the floor where the course was being held.

On my way to the course room, I remembered what had happened while waiting for the elevator to go down to Human Resources. I was not sure if it had been my imagination. It was the first time I had felt that way. Before, I had what I called hunches, like when a professor would not come to class or when my friends would call me to go out that night, and I would say no. I did not give them much importance, and as a child, I called it my spider sense. But this was different. Did I imagine it, or could I feel Jimena's heart? Yes, it was her heart. There was something else. I felt it as a noble, tender, good, straightforward, pure heart.

It had me perturbed for a moment. I accepted that it was my imagination, but at other times, I could feel her heart inside me and an odd connection. But if it was her heart, why was it racing? I stopped thinking about it; they had to be my own ridiculous thoughts.

The course started. There were twelve of us, plus two instructors and two assistants who said they were from Human Resources. It was a very intense morning, during which they gave us three massive folders with over 250 pages each, a laptop, and other material from the law firm. The folders were for the course, and they contained materials to study and exercises to do in class. We had to read and learn it all in the next two weeks, including Saturdays. They warned us that we would be working late every day to cover the course material. We started at 8 am from Monday to Saturday, and we didn't know what time we would finish.

We had an hour for lunch and two 15-minute breaks, one in the morning and one in the afternoon. The rest of the time was for studying and practicing the exercises, which were simulations of cases in international, commercial, maritime, and criminal courts. It was like going back to university, and all in 12 days. I understood now about the salary.

I was not going to have time for anything in the next two weeks, and who knew if in the next 100 years. I started to wonder if I was made for this, and I also understood the message that José gave me. If you ever have doubts,do not make any decisions without talking to me first,-my little grasshopper.- It was like it was all a trap to have new slaves in the 21st century.

I calmed down and started taking it easy. Maybe it wasn't so bad. The instructors looked very committed and happy, and although my classmates seemed to all come from high society, they didn't show it and were focused on their tasks. I could not be the only one who really needed the job to give up. Plus, there was a very important factor: Jimena. Although I did not know how I was going to see her again during these two weeks of Chinese torture, I had to persevere. She had gotten under my skin, into my mind and my body. Those minutes with her and the vision of the elevator were haunting me and making me lose concentration.

The first three days passed. I was at home on Wednesday night, and everyone was asleep. I barely had time to tell my family how my first day went on Monday, because they were all waiting for me. But I warned them not to wait for me on the following days. They were very happy, and I did not even tell them about the salary I was going to earn. I saw their expectant faces, but no one dared to ask. They probably thought I did not want to tell them.

While I was preparing my lunch to take with me, I planned to see Jimena again. Like the first day, she seemed to arrive at 7:45 a.m. The boss had a private elevator to his office, which I found out this morning. That is why I was inside and didn't see it pass. So, I would wait for her on the floor before she opened the office. I wanted to see her reaction to my boldness. I would keep looking for her every morning until the course was over.

That morning, I woke up earlier, got dressed, and took transportation to work when it was still dark outside. I had breakfast at a place near the building and still had to wait almost an hour in the cafeteria, which I used to study one of the folders. I went to the tower at 7:30 and went up to the 42nd floor again.

When the elevator opened at 7:45 a.m. and I saw the surprise on her face, I knew my plan was perfect. It did not matter if she told me to leave. I had already achieved my goal. There she was with another imposing skirt, this time navy blue with a white blouse and a cream-colored blazer that highlighted her figure, her bust, and curves.

-What are you doing here, Adrian? Did something happen? Do you have an appointment with the doctor? Why didn't I know? Was it yesterday?

-Good morning, Adrian. Nice to see you. How did you sleep? How have you been? How's your course going? Don't you think those are better questions?- She laughed out loud, and I felt fulfilled. That's why I came. All the effort had paid off.

-Sorry, you surprised me, and I got nervous. It's true, how are you? How's your course going? I see you don't have an appointment with the doctor.- She continued laughing, shaking her head, and with a very mischievous look as she opened the door.

-What doctor? I came to see the future. Do you think what I said was a joke? Well, think again. Unless you're already married and don't wear a ring, it won't be easy for you to get rid of me.

-What if I'm not married, but engaged? What are you going to do?- She asked me, biting her lip slightly. It was very subtle, but I almost jumped on her.

- No, that kind of commitment can be resolved more quickly. Divorce and those details are difficult, but still, I'm a lawyer and I can do it for you at a very low cost. But for the commitment, it's just cut off and that's it. It's a verbal contract without any civil or criminal consequences,- he laughed.

-Neither one nor the other. Do all lawyers have to be shameless to succeed? Is that taught in law school or is it a requirement to get in? Look, I can't let you in because you don't have an appointment, and the Doctor is already in his office. If he sees you, he'll ask me what you're doing here and I don't know what to tell him. And I don't like to be without answers for him. It turns out he's a lawyer like you.

-Alright, we can have that conversation later about the requirements for being a lawyer and how many shameless lawyers you've encountered along the way. But in the meantime, can you give me your phonenumber, so I don't have to come here every day at 7 in the morning to wait for you?

-You've been here since 7?

-A little bit earlier,- she continued to laugh uncontrollably. -It's almost time for the class. Your number?- She dictated it to me, and I memorized it. I wouldn't forget it for anything. -Goodbye, Jimena Llovera.- I waved to her that I would call or text her, she nodded and still laughing and shaking her head with her hair flying, walked away towards her work station.

From that moment on, everything started to go better for me. The course was not as boring, and even though we came from very different walks of life, my classmates were pleasant and competitive in a positive way. That is what the career was about, to do better every day. We could be competitive, but still behave like a team, without leaving anyone behind. Each one fought to stand out and take on leadership positions.

I spent my days in the course, and during lunch and in the afternoon, I would text Jimena. She always replied with a bit of delay, saying she was busy. I would come home late and not write to her much at night because we both had to get up early for work.

In the second week, at lunchtime, I went down to the firm's kitchenette and shared that hour with other workers, mostly from administration. The professionals did not usually eat there unless they had to stay for some work-related reason. The good salaries they paid allowed everyone to eat at the nearby restaurants. My policy was different, to save money to share with my family.

I became friends with the photocopying manager, Roman, and the secretary in charge of the document typing department, Alicia. For some reason that I did not understand, because I felt very good and have never been one for gossip, I started asking them about Jimena. When I made the first comment, they looked at me with ridicule and left without giving me any details. The next day, I insisted, as if I did not care.

-Hey, Roman, yesterday I mentioned the name of the boss's assistant and you laughed,- Alicia looked up from her food and gave me the same look, but this time she shook her head as if asking me, -Are you going to insist?

-Roman, finish telling him before this new one crashes like the others,- she said, addressing Roman and not me.

-What are you going to tell me? Is there a mystery with that girl? She seems pretty normal to me,- I insisted on the conversation, trying to act like I didn't care. Besides, I was curious when she said -like the others,- which others?

-Don't get nervous, it's nothing out of the ordinary, just the truth,- Alicia replied. -Come on, Roman, tell him everything.

-It's nothing, Adriancito, just that this girl has everyone on the staff, the professionals, and the administration staff all twisted up, but she doesn't listen to anyone. The rumor is that she's reserved.-

-Why? Does she have a boyfriend?

-Oh no, you don't understand anything, do you?-

-I'm just trying to figure it out. How is she reserved?

-Reserved, reserved for the big guys, not for the little ones.- I felt like a punch to the stomach, I didn't see that coming.

-But how? For the bosses?

-Well, the food seems to be sitting better than your ability to guess. Yes, but not for all the bosses, just for the big boss.

-The Doctor Ariztimuño?

-I didn't hear anything. Don't speak so loud, dear, the walls have ears.

-Sorry, sorry, but by God, that's really strange, such a young woman.

-And what does that have to do with it?- Alicia intervened. -Age doesn't take away anyone's ambitions. Besides, the younger they are, the faster they want to get out of 'trouble'- - and she made the gesture of quotation marks with her hands.

-I understand,- I said, thinking about what to say. -And does everyone here know that?

-Most people know, some suspect, and others who are finding out now are making the same face you're making,- Alicia said, and both of them burst out laughing.

-Well, I have to be honest, it surprises me. From what little I've known of her; she doesn't seem like that type of woman at all. Quite the opposite.

-Hmm, and how well have you known her? How intimate?- Roman asked this time.

-No intimacy at all, just a couple of times in the boss's office. But I've always had, I don't know how to explain it, a sixth sense with people, and I'm usually right. I can read people in a few moments,- I said. With these two, I was starting to realize I needed to stay as far away as possible and be careful.

-Well,- Alicia insisted, -this time let me tell you that you're wrong. That girl is hiding something with the boss, and since there's nothing hidden under the sun, someday we'll find out, and you'll see that we were right. Mrs. Emma won't take long to come and rip out those yellow locks she has.- Alicia's animosity towards Jimena was impossible to hide, so I decided to cut the conversation off there.

-Yes - I told them - it's definitely going to happen. These things aren't hidden, and the best thing we can do is stay away before we get caught up in it, especially those of us who are just starting out.

-Exactly, you hit the nail on the head. That's what we were telling you. We watch from afar, so it's better to forget about the girl. We all look at her when she walks by because we're not going to say she's not worth looking at, but then we quickly turn away and focus on something else if we're looking for a partner.- Alicia rolled her eyes at Roman's comment. -I laughed and changed the subject.

-Hey Alicia, you know everything, tell me about the party they're inviting us to on Sunday. Can I come too?-

-So, I'm the gossip girl now?- She replied with all the coquettishness she could muster. -You can't make comments because they immediately label you.

-That's not what I meant, but okay, tell me.- And the three of us laughed.

-It's the law firm's anniversary, my darling. It's not every day that they celebrate 100 years, so they're really going all out. And of course, you're invited, we're all invited. I'm sure you've been so busy with that course, day and night, that you haven't had time to read your emails, which you really should do, by the way. You have no idea what's going on.- Alicia continued, and it seemed like she was flirting with me a bit.

-So, everyone's a boss here, huh?

-Why do you say that?- The conversation was now only between Alicia and me, with Roman as a spectator.

-Well, you're telling me to read my emails and inviting me to the party without me being formally invited.

-Oh no, don't get upset with me. You're new here, I'm not your boss, but I know a lot of things. You're invited, and that's that. And if you're dressed nicely, I might even make you my date for the day.

-Wow,- Roman exclaimed. -She's not beating around the bush, that's just how she is.- It took me a moment to react; I had been sensing it, but I didn't expect it.

-Sure, no problem. And as for dressing nicely, I always do.

-Look at him, he's so full of himself,- Alicia teased. -But seriously, you looked good in that suit.

-But why do you challenge me and then insult me?- I asked, a bit confused.

-I'm not insulting you, I'm just telling the truth. Alright, don't get mad. See you on Sunday. I have a lot of work to do.- Alicia stood up and left. Several people had been paying attention to the conversation, especially the last part. We had spoken quietly about Jimena, but the part about the party was audible to everyone else. So they laughed when Alicia got up and left, and again at Roman's next comment.

-You nailed it, bro. She doesn't mince words, but if she's going forward, you won't be able to stop her.- Everyone looked at me and continued laughing. I think I even blushed, which is very unusual for me. Alicia was an attractive woman in her early 30s with a good body, but I never thought of getting into a situation with her, especially with Jimena on my mind. I had forgotten about Jimena.

It was already Wednesday, and the course was about to end. From this day on, almost everything talked about in the office was related to the law firm's anniversary party. The instructors introduced the topic among the newbies taking the course, and that sparked questions about the dress code, time, program, and venue of the event. The women planned what they were going to wear, and the men were more focused on thinking about what to eat and drink, of course, also paying attention to how the women were goingto dress. Conversations revolved around the upcoming Sunday and consumed almost all of the time. In the afternoon before we left, they sent us the final email with the program.

It was going to be held at a hacienda on the outskirts of the city, and the firm would provide buses for all staff. The departure would be from the ground floor of the building at 9 a.m. with a return at 8 p.m., an all-day event with three meals, dancing, and entertainment. The law firm spent a lot of money to celebrate its 100th anniversary with all employees.

That day, I spent thinking about Jimena. After talking to Roman and Alicia, Icould not think of anything else. They said some very strong things about her, and not only to me, but they also claimed that it was common knowledge in the company.

With all this on my mind, Idid not write to her in the afternoon when I left the course, and I didn't do it at night as I usually did since she gave me her phone number. I checked the chat app, and she was online. What worried me and accentuated the worm of distrust injected into me was that I had asked her several times about her personal life, and she avoided me and changed the subject. We always ended up talking about me and my family, but in all these days of chatting, I did not know anything about her.

I could not find a way not to mention the topic, but I didn't feel good about myself either. What they painted for me was not what I felt for her. I couldn't imagine Jimena in a fling with Jose, not because it was something I could judge, no, those things happened in jobs all the time, and many of those cases were true love, sometimes frustrated for some reason and other times ended due to lack of courage from those involved, but other times they led to resolving marriages that were not going well, and the lovers ended a true love story. It was not that. If that was the case, then fine, but I felt that was not what was happening with Jimena and Jose.

I could not interpret it rationally, but I was sure that the time I felt her heart, the connection was very strong, and maybe I was wrong and wanted to believe what my mind was telling me to believe, but then where did I get that softness, those startled heartbeats, and that vision of her looking at me from the depths of her soul?

I do not think it was just my mind, there was something else and I had to know what was driving me to not believe in all those comments that now seemed unhealthy and very ill-intentioned. You cannot judge people without knowing their situation, without understanding what they're going through, without understanding where they come from and what motivates them.

I spent Thursday morning in the course and at noon, I did not go to the kitchenette for lunch. I went down to a square in front of the building and ate a sandwich I had prepared. Between the intensity of the course and not knowing what to write to Jimena, I had lost my appetite.

Suddenly, I saw her enter the building. It was impressive to see her walk from afar, with her skirt and high heels, her body swayed from side to side and the sway was intoxicating. I now understood very well the reason for the envy of other women and the need that this feeling has to hurt the subject who receives it.

For a moment, I felt really bad for letting myself be influenced and reacted. I could not continue with this ambiguity. I knew very well that I had felt her heart. I had no more doubts, and if there was something between her and her boss, it was not my problem. After all, he got there first, and she had every right to have a relationship with whomever she wanted. It was not me who could judge her, and even less judge him. Jimena was an impressive woman, and anyone could easily be captivated by her. Look at me, for example.

I waited for her to have time to reach her office and I wrote to her. I wanted to know how she had been, but above all, if she had missed me not writing to her the day before.

-Hey Jimena, how are you?- I started.

-But how dry, and after forgetting about me for more than 24 hours, you greet me like that?- I didn't expect that response, but as soon as I sent the message, I regretted the greeting. It wasn't the way I started writing to her every time I did in the previous days.

-You're right, doll, sorry, but I've been very busy. We're almost done with the course.

-Okay, but what about the 24 hours?- She kept complaining. We had been very friendly and affectionate in the messages of the previous days, but this reaction was much more than I expected. My heart started beating fast, and my mind was clouding up to answer her.

-It wasn't exactly 24 hours.

-Twenty-five.

-Hahaha, okay, 25, since yesterday noon until today's noon, approximately.

-Not exact, so you know how long it's been since you wrote to me.

-Well, but I already wrote to you, and I also wanted to let you rest from this boy, you don't get bored and leave me on the side.

-That wasn't it, did something happen?

-Nothing, just between the course and having to go buy clothes for Sunday, it's really hectic. Did you already buy yours?

-I'm just arriving. I did it in record time.

-And what did you buy? Send me pictures.

-Hahaha, you're going too far, no way, it's a surprise. - I felt relieved that she had forgotten about the abandonment issue, and I didn't have to mention the unhealthy conversation we had yesterday.

-But a sneak peek, like they call it a -preview.

-Nope, forget it. You have to wait until Sunday. Are you going, right?

-Of course, I didn't tell you that I was already planning on it yesterday. - I felt panicked after finishing writing. It would be on Saturday afternoon that I could go buy something to wear if we had time after the course, because I really didn't have any clothes for a countryside day.

-And how much did you buy for the day and to change?

-What???

-Of course, what do you think? You're not going to spend the whole day in the same clothes, you have to change. It's obvious...

-I hadn't thought of that.

-I thought you would have good advisors down there, and I said to myself, that's why he hasn't written to me anymore.

-Oh my god, but you hadn't forgotten that part already, had you?

-No, nothing escapes me, what do you think?

-You're going to have to accompany me - I said to her, it was my opportunity.

-When?

-It'll be on Saturday because before that it's impossible. And on Saturday afternoon, after the course, as soon as I get in, I'll start working on leaving early on Saturday, so we have time. I'll tell the women to start asking the instructors.

-You're dangerous, you know how to manipulate people. I'm going to start getting scared of you.

-I'm going to completely ignore that comment and let's focus on the fact that I have to go. Saturday at 5 pm down there at the entrance of the building.

-No, not at the entrance of the building, let's meet at the Mall.

-Okay, you wait for me at the Mall and I'll text you as soon as I'm out. Anyway, we'll plan it better tonight.

-Okay.

I was left thinking, oh my god, why are humans like this? That refusal to meet at the entrance of the building was what made me doubt, I did not understand. Was she scared of being seen with me? If she had nothing to hide, why couldn't she leave with me from the law firm's headquarters? What was stopping her from leaving with me from the building?

I had to get to the bottom of this, I didn't know how to do it, but the worst thing for a relationship, especially in the beginning, is doubt. You cannot build anything on thoughts that assault you and make you change your mind. You seem crazy, bipolar, one moment you are euphoric with love and passion and the next moment you want to get away and never see her again, or worse, make her suffer like you're suffering, but without telling her why, without being brave enough to confront the real reason causing the discomfort. You do not dare to tell her because something in you tells you it's not true, that if you tell her, you'll offend her and lose her, and you keep suffering alone and hurting her in the process.

I did not want this to happen to me. At the first opportunity I had, I was going to ask her, I was going to tell her everything I had heard, without trying to make her feel bad, but I had to clarify, I had to know, but I also had to trust myself, I had to trust what my inner self was telling me, in the communication I had felt with her.

The three remaining days of the course passed, and we ended with a small toast. The instructors told us that traditionally we went out at night with the new assistants and associates and shared in a club or restaurant, whatever the group chose, but as tomorrow was the law firm party, this time itdid notapply to us.

What we insisted on was that we were owed it and that we would all go out together in a week or two. My idea of being allowed to leave early was perfectly received by the group and the instructors, so we finished before 3 pm, had a glass of champagne to toast the success of the course and our future performance as lawyers, and were wished a long career by the two associates who taught us the program. We said goodbye affectionately and gave a gift to each of the professors.

They received it with great excitement, theydid not expect it. It was the idea of one of the girls in the group who had a lot of money, and very good taste, which I deduced from the instructors' faces when they opened the gift and the portion of the fine that fell to me to pay for those gifts.

The moment I had been waiting for so long had arrived, I was finally going out with Jimena. I wrote to her all the time trying not to be seen, she was teasing me and wrote back several times pretending to be angry because I did not return her messages promptly and then laughed at my reaction, supposedly to calm her discomfort.

I called her when I got down to know where she was, took the first taxi I saw to the mall and found her sitting in a café eating a cookie and ice cream. She got up to greet me with a kiss, but I had time to observe her well. If I thought she looked impressive dressed in skirts for work, I was far from imagining how she looked in casual clothes, as simple as with tight jeans on her body, a short blouse that barely covered her belly button and highlighted her bust to the point of seeming to protrude too muchfrom her chest, high-cut athletic shoes that made her legs look eternal, hair completely loose, and only lipstick as makeup. I was left ecstatic and speechless for a few seconds that seemed excessive to her.

I kissed her and brushed her cheek, it was the softest and most delicate thing I had ever felt in my 25 years, the contact with her skin injected a warmth into me that I would need for the rest of my life. I felt a shiver run through my entire body and I could see that she also trembled. It was only a moment, but I think I saw it. She smiled at me and brought me back to reality.

-Have you been waiting for long?- she asked.

-No, just a little bit. I took the opportunity to eat the strawberry ice cream with cream that I like, and the waiter gave me this cookie.- When I turned my head, I could see the waiter looking at us with a mix of mischief and jealousy. I felt a surge of pride and took her hand.

-Have you paid already?- I asked.

-Yes.

-Then let's go, because last time I came here, I couldn't buy anything. We hadn't been paid yet, and I didn't have much time, so I just looked around.- I had to invent that little lie because I needed to buy two changes of clothes, and I had already told her that I had left earlier. I looked back at the waiter as we walked away, and he was still watching us. I imagine seeing Jimena walking away must havebeen quite a spectacle. I would take a moment to do it myself.

-And do you plan to hold my hand as if we were dating?- she said, looking directly at our intertwined hands and laughing.

-Well, yeah, I don't mind at all.- On the contrary, I still felt that warmth invades me with her touch.-If it bothers you, you'll have to appeal to the judge of the case, but I inform you that at this time on Saturdays, all the courts are closed.

-Then I'll have to go to the Administrative Judge of the plaintiff's domicile,- she said in immediate response. I looked at her in surprise and suddenly let go of her hand.

-Miss, you just recited a part of the law. How do you know that? Did you learn it in your boss's office?- She laughed mockingly.

-Now an assistant can't know the law because he surprises Don Lawyer?

-No, it's not that. The answer is very accurate, it has nothing to do with the game I played with you. Tell me, I want to know, I want to know everything about you, Jimena.- I said this with a slightly shaky voice. What I was feeling was growing exponentially every second I was with her, and I didn't want to crash -like the others,- according to Roman and Alicia's argument.

-Little by little, Adrian, I'll tell you, but don't let go of my hand because you're afraid of what you don't know about me.- She offered me her hand, and I gently took it. I felt the connection with her heart again, I looked into her brown eyes and saw a hint of sadness. I felt her nobility and transparency. I squeezed her hand, and we continued walking, looking at the shop windows. I thought about the tone in which she spoke, and she seemed like a very old woman, a very wise woman, beyond what was understandable for a person her age.

-What did you see when you came?- she asked.

-Nothing, really. Like I said, I just looked around, and I didn't like anything. I didn't even know what my budget was.

-That's true, those parties make you have to spend money on clothes that you don't know when you'll wear again.

-So, let's buy some swimsuits and show up at the party like that. I assume that the estate has a pool or at least a water tank to bathe in.

-And I imagine that you guys at the law firm spent the whole week making plans to see all the women in swimsuits, right? Well, no. There's a pool, but no one is going to swim, no sir.

-Don't get mad, that was just something I made up right now, we didn't talk about any of that.

-And what did you say? I believed you.

-I'm serious, jealous lady. I haven't thought about that at all. It was just a thought I had about seeing you in a swimsuit.

-Don't change the subject. Who knows who you wanted to see in a swimsuit if you spent two weeks in that jungle.- This time it was me who burst into uncontrollable laughter. I didn't know this Jimena, she said all that with the pouty face of a spoiled and jealous girl that aroused all my masculinity.

-Okay, let's do something, we buy the swimsuits and hide and bathe ourselves alone, what do you think, just us.

-Stop it, you're going to annoy me. There are no swimsuits, nobody's going to buy them, and nobody's going to wear them.

-Can you tell me exactly what you know that I don't know? - I asked her, because I felt there was something serious in the jokes, she was making with me.

-That's exactly what I'm asking you. Can you tell me exactly what you did down there in the jungle and want to repeat in my apartment? - She was starting to get serious.

-What if we sit down and talk honestly, don't you think?

-Sounds good to me. - I looked at her and she gestured for me to start.

-I'm going to talk without knowing what they've told you, because it seems that's what we both have, stories, because I also have my part that I've been carrying for several days.- I started trying to choose my words with the greatest care. I didn't want to hurt her, being with her I was sure that what they told me was false, but if I told her, it could put her in a position where she wanted to make a decision regarding her stay inthe firm based on what others thought and said about her.

-I know what they told you, but that doesn't concern me.- Then she knew about the conversation in the kitchenette, then she also knew about the direct attack Alicia made on me. I felt immense relief at what that meant. She had just said that what they told her about me didn't concern her, so it couldn't be true, or if it was true, what was it? I decided to be as honest as possible without hurting her.

-Look, Jimena, what I have at the firm is two weeks and I don't know anyone and I don't know the informal culture of the organization, but what little I've been able to perceive, because that's the correct word, I see it in people's faces, in their gaze, even in the way they walk and gesture, there's like a flow of feelings that leads people to act wrongly. That flow may be perhaps some injustice that was committed sometime in the organization and has been passed down from generation to generation and has not healed individually or collectively. That is, the solidarity generated by the injustice in the group because of individual harm has been transferred to different layers of professionals who come in and out of the company. This generates any wrong feeling in the group and brings out the worst in each human being who is linked to that injustice. So, envy, personal and professional jealousy, gossip, slander, it's all part of the same thing and we don't necessarily have to take it personally. It's not about us, it's not our responsibility, we have to leave it to that injustice, to the fact and to the people who generated it, who knows how many times ago. This is an organization that will celebrate its 100th anniversary tomorrow.

-What do you mean by that?

-I mean that nothing that I have heard or seen in these two weeks is within my understanding because I don't know the stories, I haven't participated in them, and it would be a grave mistake if I get caught up in one of them and fall into the same dynamicsin which everyone is immersed. Alicia may be one more victim of those struggles, of those stories.

-Alicia, a victim?-He smiled bitterly, the first time I saw that gesture.

-Yes, unfortunately, we are all victims and victimizers at the same time. When you are hurt, in order not to sink into pain, you need compensation. And if you don't have the person who inflicted the pain on you nearby to pay them back, or because of love you don't want to harm them directly, you will seek compensation with the person closest to you who is most similar to you. You need to know that there is someone as or more vulnerable than you. That's why I deduce, not that I know, that Alicia and some others there are victims who have suffered some harm or are reflecting the inherited pain of someone who preceded them.

-How can you know that?

-I don't know, I told you, it's like an understanding that came to me suddenly trying to understand why there can be these relationships and feelings between people who are obliged to get along well if they want to obtain the professional, personal, and financial success that an entity like the one we work for requires.

-So, you have nothing with Alicia? - The question was too innocent, too soft, and sweet, I couldn't understand how there were people who could judge her without knowing her - because I have nothing with Doctor Ariztimuño, as you call him, with José.

-Why do you tell me that?

-Because that's what they told you, they've been saying it for two years, since I arrived at the law firm, but I don't care, it doesn't affect me, but they told you and you must have believed it because you didn't write to me that afternoon. And you didn't answer me about Alicia.

-Let's take it step by step, okay? No, I don't have, nor will I ever have, anything with Alicia, it's impossible for many reasons, the main one I think you already know. If I didn't write to you, it was because of what they told me, it affected me, it affected me a lot, but then I remembered that since the first day we talked, I'm going to tell you something, please don't laugh, I felt it, I felt your heart beating, more than feeling attracted to you, I felt connected to you. I don't know how to explain it, but that's what I've been experiencing since that day, and it's different. It's not like anything before. Women usually like you, attract you, but don't connect with you, they are different things. That's why it affected me more than normal. It's not the same to hear a rumor about a pretty, young woman than to hear it about the woman who, without having talked enough with her, you believe you know better than anyone because you felt her.

There was silence between us. We were surrounded by many people in the mall, we were sitting next to a couple who had two small children running around and screaming, but the silence was profound. Our gazes remained motionless, fixed on each other, for several seconds that seemed like an eternity. I was transported to a place where I felt very safe, very calm, a place full of love and peace, warm, full of light and happiness. Suddenly, Jimena stood up, took my hand, and started to walk.

-Let's go shopping because they are going to close and tomorrow, we have to wake up early and you haven't bought anything, I'll choose everything,- she said quickly and started walking straight to the stores that she had apparently chosen beforehand.

-But you already know where we're going, right?

-What do you think I did while waiting for you? I already know everything you're going to wear, and please, don't be stingy this time,- she said as if she knew that part of me.

-I'm not stingy,- I protested. But I was, I have experienced scarcity a lot and the technical term wasn't stingy, but cautious.

-Yes, you are. You say you connect with me, so what do you think? I knew you before you even arrived at the law firm.

-How is that? Tell me.

-Not today, there will be time to tell you later. Today, we're going to spend that first paycheck they deposited,- she laughed spontaneously and sincerely, maybe because of the idea of spending it, and it started to worry me.

We went to all the stores she had planned; some were very expensive, the others were fine. I flatly refused to buy anything in the expensive stores, not even a pair of socks, so I ended up buying at the department stores, mostly at her suggestion. I had to try on the clothes and come out of the dressing room for her approval, it became a delicious game of complicity. Each disapproving or approving look was a flame of mischievousness and connection. I felt her flirting as a beautiful and honest woman, a noble and upright woman. We walked hand in hand, went back to eat ice cream, had coffee, and ended up having a quick and healthy dinner at the food fair.

While having dinner, we made the plan for tomorrow. We had to synchronize our arrival at the headquarters building because the staff would start boarding the bus as they arrived, and each unit would leave when it was full. If we wanted to go together, we had to arrive almost at the same time. My suggestion was that I would take a taxi and pick her up at her house. At first, shedid not want to accept, but after insisting so much, and I think mostly to avoid so many questions from me about why she didn't want me to go to her house, she ended up accepting as a sign of trust and that there was nothing to hide from her part. The second question was more difficult, were we going to sit together and make the 45-minute trip sitting together? The answer was simple, yes.

-I already told you that I don't care what they say about me, unless you don't want your Alicia to see us,- I laughed.

-Is that a joke, right? I don't feel you like a jealous woman, and besides, that's already cleared up.

-I'm joking, don't be delicate,- she looked at me very sweetly and melted all my defenses.

-Don't do that.

- What thing?

- Looking at me like that, we're in a public place.

- Ok, I won't look at you anymore- and he turned his face away.

- Don't ever stop looking at me, that's all I'm going to ask of you, don't ever take your eyes off me, it's the only condition for whatever you and I can be in the future.

- Maybe nothing.

- It doesn't matter, maybe nothing, but don't stop looking at me, ok?

- Ok.

We got up and started walking towards the mall exit, slowly, holding hands and in silence, our first date, our first day together had ended.

Neither of us wanted it to end, we knew that when we got outside each one would take a taxi home, we had already discussed it, how we would say goodbye, if I would accompany her to her house and she told me no, that tomorrow I would know where she lived and would see her house, that she had to get her clothes and suitcase in order for the next day and that I had to do the same, iron the new clothes because if not my coworkers would make fun of me, there was work to be done.

Every step we took felt like we were getting further away from each other, there was no kiss and there would not be, tacitly without speaking, we knew it, I didn't want to force what we had advanced today and she wasn't the one to take the first step.

We reached the exit and the taxis lined up to pick up passengers, I accompanied her to the first one in line and we stood looking at each other, very closely, fixedly staring into each other's eyes, the moment of tension grew, I approached and kissed her on the cheek, she rested her face on mine for a moment and I felt her fresh and fleshy lips deposit a long kiss on my cheek, and a sigh escaped from our chests. She got into the car without turning to look at me and drove away.

I got home, ironed the clothes I was going to wear, prepared my bag for the next day and went to bed early, but it was a long night, I woke up several times with my mind set on going to look for Jimena, going to the reception together and imagining spending the whole day showing her off in front of everyone.

One of the times I fell deeply asleep I dreamed that we were arriving at a place that looked like a jungle or a very dense forest, in the middle of that forest there was a clearing and I saw a very long rectangular construction that had a staircase in thecenter.

Jimena was walking with me, I could sense her presence but couldn't see her next to me. It was more like I could feel her gaze on my back, but I tried to grab her hand and she was not there. We continued walking towards the construction site, and the staircase changed direction and we started going down. Each step we took made the staircase narrower, more humid, and darker. Suddenly, I entered a large room that projected a dim light coming from high chandeliers arranged around the walls. Jimena was at the back of the room waiting for me, her head tilted back as if looking up at the ceiling. She extended her hands and called out to me. I turned to see if she was still by my side, but shewas not. She was in front of me, asking me to come closer, but I could not seem to find a way to reach her. Every step I took inside the room made the distance between us greater. I stopped so she would notget further away, and then she looked me straight in the eyes and held my gaze, like we had done earlier when we were sitting and talking at the mall. I saw the saddest face I had ever seen, but at the same time, she exuded a celestial beauty that was hard to describe.

I woke up startled, sweating and gasping for air. I felt the suffocation of the depth of having gone down the stairs into the ground, even though I had never been claustrophobic before. Jimena's gaze made me want to cry, and it was difficult to contain my sorrow. I gradually recovered, looked outside and saw that it was dawn. It was still more than an hour before the alarm clock would go off to wake me up, but I got up, showered, dressed, and made myself a cup of coffee, waiting for the time to go and find her.

I had time to go over the dream or nightmare several times; it wouldn't leave my mind, especially because I remembered all the details, and I didn't know how long it had lasted. To me, it seemed like an eternity, everything I had experienced. I felt the pain in her gaze, the suffering that was visible, isolated and distant.

I ordered the taxi with enough time to let her know I was on my way to her house, which was about a twenty-minute ride, but I didn't want to rush her. From my previous relationships, I knew that women need their time to get dressed on a party day, so I texted her without expecting a response, as it indeed happened, and talked to the driver to be patient and wait for her.

I arrived at the front of her house, which was a small house with a fence made of blocks that were no more than 90 centimeters high, continuing with an ornamental wrought iron that simulated long-petal rosettes. It had a small garden in the center with red cayenne and white lilies, surrounded by a bright green grass that made the yellow color of the rose path to the house door stand out.

It looked like the entrance to a countryside drawing in the middle of the city. I pictured Jimena passing by that entrance every day, and everything made sense. It perfectly matched the image of her that I had, a subtle and beautiful angel walking on a flower path towards her dwelling.

I woke up from the dream with a start, and I think the taxi driver let out a whistle, but I am not sure. What came out of the door was not an angel precisely. She wore a tight white short and a sleeveless blue floral blouse that left all the skin around her arms and bust exposed. Her curly brown hair cascaded in torrents over her shoulders and back and swayed with each step. Her high-cut sports shoes made her legs look spectacular.

I got off the front seat of the car, opened the door for her, she got in, and I followed. I greeted her with a kiss, and I did not know how to start the conversation. Something inside me beat with great force, and I could not control it. I could not take my eyes off her legs, toned, firm, and thicker than usual, with skin that seemed extremely soft. I felt like I was melting in the car seat.

- So, what do you tell the kids, did the mice eat your tongue or are you still asleep?

- Neither one nor the other. But I'll be supremely honest with you, you left me speechless, you're more than beautiful and provocative, I have no words. I think I'll tell the driver to take us somewhere else.

- But what's happening to you? I don't know you like this; you're acting weird - she said, laughing nervously. I think she didn't know if I was serious or joking.

- You know I'm joking, but I really want it to be true.

- No, no, apologize, that was very rude.

- Ok, sorry, let's start over. Forget about the past. Jimena, how are you? How was your night? You look really beautiful in that outfit. I really like your combination.

- I'm doing great, thank you. Very grateful for the compliment so early in the morning - she replied slowly, laughing.

- What I can add is that you look good enough to eat.

- But are you going to keep going? If you do, I'll tell the driver to stop and I'll get off.

- If you get off, I'll get off with you and we'll run away and nobody pays.

- I'm listening - the driver said. The truth is that it was a very small car and no matter how quietly we spoke, everything could be heard. We all burst out laughing.

- Alright, I'll behave - I agreed.

- All day - she added.

- What do you mean, all day?

- Yes, you're going to behave like a gentleman, with me obviously, all day no matter what you see.

- So, there's more? This isn't the only or the best thing? Is that what you're trying to tell me?

- I'm not trying to tell you anything, just repeat the phrase and commit to it.

- Committed, completely and only with you. Is that okay?

- Okay.

We kept chatting in the same tone as we rode towards the law firm's headquarters. I could not get her to tell me what the reason was for the commitment she had just made, nor if there was a bigger surprise than the white shorts. We arrived relatively quickly for my liking, I paid the driver and we got off. We saw the bus at the entrance of the building and headed straight to the line that was formed at the door of the vehicle to board.

As soon as we approached, everything changed. We felt the stares of those who were about to board and some who were already on board, Jimena caused a commotion, no one had ever seen her with a similar outfit, the men did not conceal their admiration until the indiscretion of wanting to see through what she was wearing, and the women tried to hide it, but without exception they all turned to minutely examine how each piece she was wearing looked, if it matched, and how it looked specifically on her. When they conversed with the person next to them, it was evident that they were commenting on their impressions of Jimena.

I glanced at her sideways and saw her raise her chin and sigh, gathering strength to walk dignifiedly among so many gazes. She did it like a queen, not looking directly at anyone and continuing until we found a couple of seats at the back of the unit to sit together. I had disappeared, I hardly knew anyone who got on with us and therefore assumed that I would be a stranger to them too, but more than that, I realized that no one took me into account, as if she had entered alone and I did notexist. Once we were seated, I told her:

-Did you feel that?

-Shh – she made a vertical finger signal on her lips and looked at me lovingly. - You have to get used to it, I'm sorry for putting you in this, but it's my day to day. - She said in a very low voice and caressed my hand and withdrew it very quickly, we continued talking almost whispering with our faces very close, which I liked very much.

-It was intense, it wasn't with me, and I could feel it as if I had been searched by the police when they stopped me drunk on the street with my friends, the men undressed you and the women dismembered you, to say something mild. - I insisted.

-Drunk?

-My god, woman, focus, it was just a saying.

-No, if today has been revealing, I'm getting to know you. - I couldn't help but laugh and she joined me, I think I understood that she didn't want to know anything about the topic. She looked at me, moved her face away, and we continued talking loudly, while the bus started and drove away from the city on the highway towards where the reception to celebrate the 100 years of Ariztimuño & Fermonsel Law Firm would take place.

We got off the highway and the road became narrower and uphill, we entered a mountainous area, with beautiful landscapes, it was going to be a sunny and clear day.

We talked as much as we could out loud, just work nonsense, she gave me several tips on how to behave in front of the group of partners, she named them all, highlighting only the positive attributes that each one had, I understood that any adverse comment would reach the partner's ear before we got off the bus.

Between each comment, she made all kinds of gestures to let me know that what she was saying was not entirely true, and I would burst out in contained laughter, which would earn me either a pinch or a beautiful scolding expression. Whenever I complained about either one, the dose was repeated.

This Jimena was a hundred times better than I had imagined. If I thought I could fall in love with her, being with her made me soar to heights that were very easy to get used to and never wanted to come down from.

We arrived at the gate of the Hacienda, and the driver took a few minutes to park and prepare to open the door, which allowed us all to take a good look at the place, and the murmurs of admiration were widespread.

It was an impressive place, and the morning sun highlighted the perfect cut green of the lawn that extended throughout the area, between hills and mountains that reached as far as the eye could see. The entrance was a giant arch of limestone, and there were several paths to what appeared to be the clubhouse, one was made of ochre-colored cobblestones, another of white stones and cut logs, with grass and small shoots of violets and geraniums.

We began to get off, with us being the last since our seats were at the back, we picked up our bags, and when we got off the bus, I felt there was a waiting procession for Jimena, arranged so that nobody missed seeing her well.

She behaved in the same way, but I could not help but look everyone in the face and greet them as if I knew them. There were people from both the professional staff and administration, some of whom I remembered seeing in the elevator or in the kitchenette. My attitude was successful, and although they returned the greeting politely, they felt included and disengaged from the matter, or so it seemed.

We realized that our bus was the third to arrive, and two others were already parked, and the fourth was arriving behind us, meaning that there were already almost two hundred people at the Hacienda.

-Come, I have a better and more beautiful way to get to the clubhouse,- Jimena said to me.

-How is that? Have you been here before?- I asked.

-Of course, I helped choose the site. Who do you think is the assistant to the main partner?- she replied, boasting of her position and influence. She took a path next to the parking lot that descended into the terrain, lost in a path covered entirely with bamboos. The sunlight barely penetrated, and the humidity made the path feel very fresh. We walked hand in hand very slowly, with nobody around. The music at the clubhouse was heard in the distance, passing over the bamboo plants and blending with the sound of the leaves rustling in the wind.

-Don't take what I'm about to say the wrong way, I know it's all slander,- I began. -But don't you think that, in addition to your indifferent attitude towards all these people, not that it justifies them, and your trusting relationship with José Ariztimuño, things are getting a bit out of hand?

-Adrian, don't worry about me, I'm really okay, there's nothing to worry about, those people can't hurt me if that's what you're worried about. I can't change who I am, and I can only continue on my path until I achieve everything I want.-

-I don't understand, your words confuse me even more. As far as I can see, you're the most wonderful woman I know, the sweetest and most angelic, innocent and noble, how can other people not notice it. And on the other hand, I don't know what path you're referring to or where it leads. Can you explain it to me so I can stop worrying? Because, as you say, I do worry. It's not for nothing, in the history of humanity, there are thousands of examples of how man's incomprehension has destroyed innocent lives and entire civilizations, how can I not feel afraid of what might happen to you when the energy of hundreds of people, like the ones I can see, is all directed against you?

-You told me that at some point you felt my heart,- I nodded, I didn't remember telling her-Well, right now I've felt yours, and I know that what you said to me is totally sincere, and I appreciate it more than you can imagine. There are few people with whom I've been able to feel this connection. I thank you very much for your concern, but I repeat, I'm okay, and I feel that they can't hurt me. We have a lot of time to talk today, and I promise you that you will know everything,- she said with solemnity. I was surprised that she announced that she would tell me everything. What could it be? I felt like the world was spinning. I hoped it wasn't anything related to that hateful and ugly rumor that was on everyone's lips. Because you're going to stay with me, right? You're not going to go with your Alicia? She let go of my hand and went running for the remaining stretch of road to the clubhouse exit. I almost caught up with her, but suddenly we came face to face with the rest of the staff, who were already taking their places in the various parts of the hall.

I watched her as she crossed the hall and headed towards the Hacienda's offices. She spoke to one or two people, gave instructions here and there. As she did all this, it was as if an electric bolt had passed through the general hall. People chatted among themselves, but from one second to the next, they directed their gaze towards her. I could not deny that they were right; she was by far the most beautiful and youngest woman at the meeting. Her body was impressive, her freshness, her curly hair falling from side to side, her small hip cladsin shorts that made her backside stand out too much, her long legs perfect in their shape, round and thick, but above all, her ease in speaking, directing and giving orders at her young age.

I could not criticize them, she was there and very distant for everyone, but very close to me. I started to think about it, how was it that with so little time in the organization and knowing her, I was in the position I was in and all these people who had known herfor two years, including the men who were enamored with her, were so far away? Destiny? Luck?

-Adrian, Adrian,- I heard behind me it was Alicia and Roman approaching.

-Hi Alicia, hey Roman, how are you? Are you arriving?

-No, we came on the first bus, do you think we're going to miss a single second of all this? - Román replied.

-Of course not, my dear, but look how handsome this boy is, I already have someone to dance with all day. Alicia secured a dance partner for herself without giving me a chance to react.

Several people from the administration and my course-mates approached, a group of eight to ten people formed, all talking at the same time. One topic did not end before another was brought up or two or three topics were discussed simultaneously. I looked over the shoulder of the person in front of me and saw Jimena giving instructions to some waiters. She looked at me sharply and coldly, the group became lively and grew to more than twenty people as we introduced ourselves. Some of them had come with us on the bus and greeted me again, others seemed to want to bring up a topic but could not find the right moment to introduce it. Until a tall, dark young man who said he was a second-year assistant and named Jorge Quintero looked at me and stopped the conversation.

-And you just arrived, and you're already tangled up with the boss's girlfriend? - There was a deep silence, no one continued talking and everyone turned to look at me, waiting for my response. My blood boiled immediately and Urriaga was about to make a scene. In an instant, I imagined punching him directly in the face, but in the next instant, I remembered when Jimena told me to lower my voice on the bus and gently brushed my hand. Remembering the sensation of her skin calmed me down, and I responded witha sarcastic tone.

-I touched you on the lower back a while ago and you didn't even realize it, just to show you how fast I am,- I said. Everyone burst out laughing and the teasing had the desired effect. We changed the topic and continued with a variety of subjects, jokes, and nonsense. But I noticed that Jorge was affected by the joke and walked directly over to where Jimena was sitting. I thought he was going to talk to her, but at the last moment he changed direction, after taking a close examination of the merchandise. Later, Alicia approached me and took me away from the group by the arm. At that moment, Jimena looked at me and went to sit at one of the low tables that were around the main room, where there were high lounge tables in the middle and low ones close to the walls.

-You're not going to leave me hanging, are you? I've been keeping you for me for over a week. Besides, forget about that girl. She only has eyes for the bosses. Look!- she said, not even bothering to conceal where Jimena was sitting. We saw one of the Partners, the youngest and most eligible bachelor in the firm, approach her. -Do you see? And what were you thinking? That she was going to pay attention to you, the new guy who just arrived?- For a moment, I was speechless. I was not naturally jealous, but the thought of someone approaching her with romantic intentions, especially someone with a privileged and much superior position to mine, caught me off guard.

-See, it's a good thing you reconsidered,- Alicia stated.

-Why do you say that I reconsidered?

-Because I know when a man feels jealous like you're feeling right now, and also because you don't stand a chance sinceshe's interested in this guy who looks lost but who's actually the boss.- Everything she said was too much, it made me feel terrible, and I couldn't understand how this negative energy was taking hold of me. I took a deep breath and overcame it. It was very different when I was with her, none of this was real, it felt so ugly and low, but when I was with her, I felt like I was in heaven, and that was what I wanted.

-Thanks, Alicia, this conversation has been very enlightening, I really appreciate it,- I told her and I moved away from her. I slowly began to walk towards where Jimena was, without taking my eyes off her. She looked at me fixedly, almost counting the steps I was taking. She stood up slowly and almost cut off the conversation with the partner she was sitting with. She took two steps in my direction and approached me, almost brushing against my chest.

-Don't leave me alone in this room again,- I told her.

-Don't leave me alone in this room again,- she replied, shaking her head from side to side. I lifted her chin,and her eyes were moist.

-No, no more. I don't care what they say anymore, there's no way to please them.

-Understood, that's good.

-I understand that everyone sees things from their own perspective, their own experience, their own pain. It's not because they're bad by nature but understanding others' situations is not humans' strong suit. We lack empathy, and we prefer to judge and sentence others to what we would never accept for ourselves. I understand that but experiencing it firsthand is something else. I think I lack the fortitude to endure it, maybe later in life with more experience.

-I don't think it's necessary to go through that, it's better not to look at it and let them be the ones to live their own hell.

-It's another option, but you would be missing out on sharing with many people by not sharing in their pain. Jimena, we're all made of a portion of pain and a portion of love, I don't know if it's fair to separate those who have more pain and only prefer those who can give us love.

-That's not what I meant, on the contrary, it's that when you carry a lot of pain, it's difficult to deal with the pain of others, especially when they want to hurt you even more.

-Well, that's another thing, obviously you have to try to heal your own pain before you can deal with the pain of others, I agree with you on that, but don't you think that before anything else, we should stop being bystanders here in the middle of the room, because I left Alicia and the group hanging, and you got up with that handsome and wealthy partner who almost conquered you, so they must be making a statue of us here.- She smiled again.

-So, you were jealous, that's good, I liked that, I'm going to sit with Mr. Araya again.- She replied as we walked away from the hall towards the surrounding gardens.-Because the first thing he did was go to Alicia's arms.- Then it was my turn to burst out laughing.

-So, you were jealous, then, should I go dance with Alicia all day as she asked me to?

-Don't youdare, because I won't talk to you again.

-You're very, very jealous, from what I see,- she looked at me horribly and turned her face away, and I twisted with laughter for a while. We walked down a path that led to a place with benches surrounded by orange bushes that gave off the scent of orange blossoms, you could feel the citrus and the fresh cut of the grass, we took the one with the most shade and sat down.

-Here we are away from everyone else, won't they come?- I asked.

-I don't think so, although as you saw, this path is easy to find, it doesn't lead anywhere else or to any other distraction, the signs for the events are very clear, I helped design them.

-Okay, but there might be another couple, in that office of over seven hundred employees, I don't think we're the only ones.

-Since when are you and I a couple, Mr. Urriaga?

-Since June 17 at 7:45 a.m., maybe earlier, when we talked on the phone.- She laughed, I loved making her laugh.

-You remembered the date, didn't you?

-That day when I got off the elevator, I was thinking that I wouldn't forget that date, and look, that thought was prophetic. I entered the law firm and met you, all on the same day at the same time. It's amazing how in an instant your life can change from one path to another, and how fortunate I was to be able to determine exactly when that happened. There may be other circumstances in which your life is changing, and you don't realize it or don't perceive it.

-Yes, there are moments when your life changes, you realize it, but you can't avoid it, and you feel like you're falling into an abyss that seems endless. You don't know what you're going to find at the bottom, whether you're going to shatter when you finish falling or you can land smoothly and comfortably.- Her fatalistic reflection on the same point I had brought surprised me and how she had changed it to something that sounded terrible.

-I hope you're not talking about June 17th because it would give me a lot of pain to think that meeting me brought you such a drastic thought.

-No, silly, I didn't mean it because of you. On the contrary - and she put a finger on my lips, I kissed it as sweet and tenderly as I could no, not you, you are a breath of fresh air in my life.

-Jimena- I began to speak very softly and slowly - can you finally tell me what has happened to you? What distresses you so much that, despite being such a young and jovial, intelligent, and witty woman, you suddenly have a hint of sadness and pain that transcend your heart? - She stared at me fixedly, hesitant to take a step she might regret, unsure whether to open her mystery to a person she had known for a short time but with whom she knew she had a special connection. She continued to look at me for a long time, during which out of respect for her pain, I decided to remain silent, only keeping eye contact and opening my heart with complete honesty so that she could believe in me and trust me.

-Well, if that's what you want, we have to start by introducing ourselves again - she said, suddenly standing up, looked at me from top to bottom from her position, and extended her hand as if meeting someone for the first time. I didn't understand anything, but I got up slowly and also extended my hand.

-Nice to meet you, my name is Adrián Urriaga, and nothing you say will scare me. - I said, trying to reduce the tension of what seemed to me something very theatrical. She smiled a little bitterly, held my hand firmly, and hesitated again. After a moment, she answered.

-Nice to meet you, my name is Jimena Ariztimuño Llovera, and I hope nothing I say will scare you. - I was paralyzed, not scared, but totally speechless and without a response. Daughter, wife, adopted, my mind couldn't find the answer. Say something, please she almost begged me and let go of my hand.

-It's not as bad as it seems, right? Are you Jose's daughter? Why do you have to hide it? - I approached her and hugged her. It was the first time I had her in my arms. I had lightly hugged her to kiss her when we greeted, but not like now. I held her in my arms for a good while, holding her entirely including her arms and torso. I was practically holding her up so she wouldn't fall, she rested her head on my chest, and I heard her sobbing.

-No, I'm not her daughter,- she responded with a choked voice, tears interrupting her speech.-I'm her niece.- I slowly sat her down against my will. I would have carried her the rest of the day. She could hardly hold herself up. When I placed her on the bench, I held her chin and asked, -But why are you crying? I don't understand, Jimena. I want to take away the pain you're feeling, but you have to tell me, why are you crying?- She sighed as if searching for air to release the pain and began to speak very slowly, her gaze lowered.

-Don't worry, Adrian. You, nor anyone, can take away the pain of losing my father. It's hard for me to talk about him. I won't deny that sometimes when I'm happy, like I am with you, his absence comes to mind, and I retreat a bit.

-I'm sorry, Jimena. I truly am. I didn't know.

-You have no way of knowing if I don't tell you. That's why we're here. I need to tell you. We can't keep pretending to be something we're not if you know nothing about me. You've told me everything about yourself, your life, your family, everything, even your friends. It's true, I've told you nothing, and I've wrapped myself in an aura of mystery.-

-Now I'm starting to understand why you avoided me when I asked about your family, but I don't have it clear. Why do you hide it? Why did you change your name?

-I'll tell you everything. Give me a minute to calm down and figure out where to start. You'll be the first person I tell everything to, and I want to do it with no details left out,so you don't have that look on your face when I finish. I want you to have no doubts and to decide if you want to continue pursuing me, as you've been doing since June 17th at 7:45 a.m., or maybe even before that when we spoke on the phone.- We both laughed with a fresh laugh, one that takes away tears and clears the mind, one that reconciles you with life and takes away pain and sorrow.

-You remembered the date well, didn't you?- I returned with the same laugh.

-These are your words, silly.

-Uh-huh, I believe you. If you don't stop boasting, I won't be able to hear your story.

-Tell me, Jimena, don't be afraid. I promise you two things: I'll pay attention like I've never paid attention to anything else, and two, I'll listen to you from my soul, and when you're finished, there will be no doubts or questions.

-Okay, to your first question, why did we hide it? Why did I use another name? Well, the law firm is for lawyers, and because it's so big and important, they can't employ anyone who doesn't have another relationship than being 'the partners' children' to perpetuate the name. All other relationships are prohibited from being hired, of course, that includes nieces and nephews. Only two people know about my relationship with Jose, the other main partner, and the HR Director, who is his right-hand woman.

-I see, perfect explanation and your reasons, but there's something that worries me about all of this.

-What thing?

-When you and I get married, how are we going to do it?- She burst out laughing. She was the same beautiful and happy woman that I liked so much.

-We don't know if that's going to happen. Before you and I get married, we have to be boyfriend and girlfriend.

-Thank goodness you're already thinking about all the steps we have to take. It looks like you have everything planned out,- she continued to laugh.

-Well, no, that's not what I meant.

-Uh-huh.

-Can I continue?

-Go ahead, Mrs. Urriaga.

-Oh my God, you're insufferable. How conceited.

-Is that why you like me?

-Who told you I liked you?

-He did, that gentleman over there,- I said, pointing to her back, and when she turned around, I kissed her neck. She slapped my hand away, gave me a furious look, and continued talking.

-My dad and Uncle Jose were twins, identical, exactly like two peas in a pod, Jose was my uncle and Juan was my dad, and I'm Jimena to continue the J tradition. They both studied law, and they both ended up on the Dean's list, but since they couldn't be tied, my dad came in first and my uncle in second.- Her voice began to break again. -Sorry, it's just that I don't talk about him much.

-Don't worry about me, just say whatever you want. If you need to cry, cry. Sometimes we avoid grieving for a loved one that we necessarily have to have, and what we do is make the pain deeper and deeper instead of relieving it. It's necessary to give ourselves permission to cry and suffer for our losses.- She grabbed my forearm tightly and continued.

-Both were selected to work at the law firm, but they couldn't, they were brothers, so the partners who interviewed them left it up to them to decide, and my dad let my uncle take the job. He convinced him with the argument that he didn't like corporations, that he preferred to dedicate his life to helping people who couldn't afford a good lawyer. My uncle didn't agree and took almost a month to accept the position until my grandparents intervened, which distanced them for a while but not for long. By that time, my dad had already married my mom, and I was born.

-Total happiness Jimena, went to work in what she wanted and had your mom and for sure the most beautiful baby in the world.

-If that's what he said. We always lacked money, my dad charged very little for his work, his clients were mostly people in need or low-income, those who paid, because there was a good part that were Pro-Bono jobs or non-profit entities. Anyway, the cases he handled were very recognized and well-handled, the legal community came to call them Juan The Good and José The Bad, now they don't call my uncle that out of respect, especially since my dad is no longer here. - She was already crying completely and her words were coming out interrupted, I handed her a pack of facial tissues she had in her bag.

-I was in high school - She sighed and continued speaking slowly. - when my dad was diagnosed with a rare brain tumor, I mean, I was in high school, but what I mean is that I was in class- She stopped to cry and I gave her more tissue -When I got home, they had already taken him, I went to the hospital and they wouldn't let me see him, he was in the Intensive Care Unit, my uncle was on the other side of the world at a conference, it was just my mom and me.

I went home to sleep - she continued - and my mom stayed at the hospital that night. The next day, I went to the hospital early and didn't see my mom at the door of the unit, I looked for her everywhere and I got very upset because I couldn't find her, I tried to go in and nobody told me anything, suddenly a nurse told me to look for her in the morgue, she must be there sorting out my father's affairs. That's how I found out. I couldn't see him anymore, I couldn't say goodbye, I couldn't kiss him before he left, he didn't tell me again that I was his love and his little queen. -I let her cry for a long time, with her face in her hands, long sobs escaping and her body shaking with force. I wrapped my arms around her, just as she was sitting sideways on the bench, to give her the strength she needed at this moment and that threatened to bring her down completely. Words were not necessary, just that she felt my support, that she knew I was there with her, that this was the beginning of my support, that no matter what happened, she could count on me. She gradually calmed down, and when she regained her composure, I spoke to her.

-I understand your pain, Jimena. The sudden departure of a father without having the opportunity to say goodbye and feel their last breath is not easy, especially in your case as an only child. How long has it been?-

-Six years, this year marked six years.

-Look, listen to me. If this is the first time you have spoken extensively about your father, as you say, then it's not the time for us to go into what to do with what you carry inside. The important thing now is for you to learn to bring it to the surface whenever you want and whenever you can. I'm here for you, to listen to you, to comfort you as much as you want and need. You have to go through the grief you've kept hidden for so long. You have to feel the pain that you've hidden all these years.

-Yes, Adrian, I've heard that before, but it hurts so much. I can't stand it.

-Yes, but for your own good, probably for your mom's too, but above all for you, you have to do it for yourself. You have to go through the grief. You can't keep hiding to avoid suffering. That's a defense mechanism of the self that protects you, but the truth, do you want to know the truth? The truth is that it's causing you more harm, a deeper and more lasting pain that can accompany you forever and can twist your whole life.

-How can you be so young and know and talk about all that?

-Don't trust everything I say. Sometimes I don't even know where it comes from. The words just come to me. But with you, it's different. When I'm near you, I'm almost sure that everything comes from a connection that I feel comes from your heart, but something inside me tells me it's deeper than that.

-What are you saying? I don't understand.

-You see, that's what I mean. I start talking and my only thought is you, so the ideas just come.

-It's nice that you talk to me like that. I'll try to finish telling you.

-If you want, you can leave it there. I almost understand everything.

-Not yet. The part about why I'm at the law firm is important for you to understand many things.

-Okay, if you can continue, I'm all ears. I'm here for you, as I said.

-Thank you.

-Don't thank me, the most wonderful thing that can happen to me is to have your trust and be able to serve as a vehicle for your healing.

-If you keep going, you're going to make me fall in love.

-You want more?

-Yes, more. I'll continue. My uncle couldn't make it to thefuneral, and it caused him a lot of pain, which he has carried along with mine all these years. After the funeral, he took care of us, we didn't have anyone else, he supported us for four years until two years ago when I was already advanced in law school.

-Are you in college?

-Yes, I am. That's why I had to keep going. I told him I was going to get a job and that I planned to pay off all the debt we have with him someday. My mom and I have everything written down to the last cent. It has caused him a lot of pain, but it's not fair that he had to pay for us for four years. My dad wouldn't have accepted that. There were no debts between them, they were good brothers, they loved each other very much, but we can't be a burden to him. He suggested that I work in the law firm and arranged everything with our last name and our relationship, as I told you before. That's why I don't write to you at noon because I use that time to study, and in the evenings until ten o'clock I disappear, it's not that I have a boyfriend as you've told me several times.

-It was a joke, it's just that you've taken me from one mystery to another.

-I know, that's why I don't answer you. At noon I'm studying, in the evenings I'm in class until ten. I get home at night and then I prepare everything for the next day. Saturday and Sunday, I study again and help my mom with the household chores. I don't have much time to distract myself, few parties and few friends, I have to finish the degree as soon as possible so that I can move on to the professional staff at that law firm or another one. So, now I might seem boring to you, but that's the life I have.She finished with a gesture of resignation.

-Not at all, that's how mine has been for the last five years. And how much longer do you have to go?

-Nothing, I finish in December of this year. - her mood had changed, and her face lit up when she talked about university, so I thought it best to continue with this topic to take her mind off the pain of her family history.

-And how have your classes been? Ah, no wonder you surprised me with your knowledge of the law, little lawyer.

-Don't call me that, little one. I don't think I am one. With what I read in my uncle's law firm and how I'm doing in university, I don't think I'm a little lawyer.

-Aha, let's see who's bragging now. Answer me directly, how are you doing in your classes?

-Hahaha, I'm the number one in my class. You can be envious, number two. - we both laughed again. Changing the topic had really lifted her spirits. That didn't mean that we didn't have a lot of work to do with her grief over her father.

-How do you know that I was the number two in my class? I've never boasted about it like some people out there.

-I told you, I read everything that comes across my desk and anything that goes to my uncle's desk.

-Poor man, I pity him. He doesn't have an assistant;he has a spy.

-Well, he thanks me for it because I always summarize it for him or give him my opinion on what I read. And let me tell you, it was me who told him to interview you because you reminded me so much of them both. - suddenly she fell silent as if she had said something indiscreet and looked down.

-Do you think I resemble your father? - I asked her softly with a lot of affection, feeling her love and pain once again. I held her hand in mine.

-That's not what I meant. The truth is that your story is like theirs, but you don't look like them. You're not their twin, and you're going to have a long life, God willing. - she looked up again and smiled at me, but the sadness was still there, hidden behind her eyes, sinking back into the depths of her soul.

-Let's summarize then. You're a beautiful, exuberant and dangerously intelligent woman with a double life as a secret agent who plans to become a millionaire in the short term, pay off her debts, and marry Number Two. - Now she let laughter flood her face and fill her with the vitality that I love.

-You were doing fine until you mentioned getting married.

-Okay, go live a life of debauchery with Number 2, with the uncle's and mother's approval.

-I'm 22 and I don't have to ask anyone's permission.

-Bingo.

-What, stop saying crazy things.

-What, what?

-There's no marriage, no moving in with anyone, I have a long way to go for that, first I have to get a boyfriend.

-That search is over.

-Uh-huh, okay - each response was a flirtation, one more than the other, I didn't know how long I could continue with the game and restrain myself.

-What do you want? A formal declaration and a ring? For God's sake, those things are no longer used.

-You don't use them, that's why you don't have a girlfriend, but I do. Whoever wants to marry me has to bring a ring and be very creative for me to say yes.

-I don't have a girlfriend? Do you want me to go for Alicia? Just a second, I'll be back - she got up, lunged at me in jest, I grabbed her by the waist to prevent her from moving and she was trapped in my arms, her face less than a centimeter away from mine.

I looked into her eyes, and she looked back at me very intensely, slowly lowering her eyelids, and saw her pink, plump, and moist lips, I closed my eyes and sank into them like when a comet crosses the sky heading towards merging with the atmosphere, in that second when we makea wish for having seen a light in space that can flood our life with the realization of the dream. I lost track of time, I don't know how long the kiss lasted or if anyone saw us, I surrendered and she surrendered, we were man and woman each looking for our complement. And boy did we complement each other, we gradually reacted, returning short kisses, it was no longer the long and passionate kiss, it was a series of kisses in which we tested each other's taste and returned the pleasure we had received.

-You don't have to mention anyone else - she said softly.

-It was a game, forgive me, you drove me crazy by saying you wouldn't be mine.

-I'm yours, you know it, you've known it for a long time - I hesitated for a moment because I didn't know what she meant, I understood that they weren't just words, it wasn't just talk, it was a statement with knowledge, did she mean the first day, when Ifelt her?

-What do you mean?- I asked, and she put a finger on my lips.

-You know,- was her only response. She kissed me again, then got up, took her bag and started walking towards the party. I sat there watching her slowly move away, thinking about everything that had just happened and everything I had just learned about Jimena. I also enjoyed the sight of her figure and the way she walked along the stone and grass path. She turned and beckoned me to follow her with her index finger, nothing more charming than that womanly sculpture making that gesture with a smile on her lips.

We joined the group at the Club House of the Estate, the reception was already in full swing, and all the members had arrived, including José Ariztimuño who was surrounded by a large group of employees and members chatting amicably. But as we walked into the room, he immediately set his eyes on Jimena, attracting the attention of several hundred eyes at the same time. With all that I already knew, I felt uncomfortable, with the knowledge of what the perverse minds around us were plotting that was happeningor about to happen. We approached the group and Jimena introduced me to José again.

-Do you remember Adrián, Doctor?

-Of course,I remember him. How have you been, Adrián? How were the two weeks of the course?

-Excellent, José. The whole course was very intense. It seemed like an express review of the university, but I had excellent trainers and the group is of great quality. We have a future and maybe the next partners of the firm,- there was a unanimous exclamation from those present around the partner and the majority laughed.

-That's the attitude, Adrián. I wouldn't expect any less from you,- he said, and it sounded quite sincere. He patted me on the shoulder and continued talking with the group.

It was very difficult to follow a conversation line, everyone talked and laughed with each other, and several conversations were established at the same time. Jimena stayed by my side, and from time to time, she touched my hand with her little finger. I looked at her over my shoulder, but she didn't look back at me. She was still paying attention to answering the others or to José, who addressed her every moment.

Truthfully, for a moment, I understood the others. Without knowing what I knew, it was difficult not to think well of the two of them. She spoke, and he looked at her with admiration. It was evident that he loved her very much, and his energy towards her was protective, like that of a father with his beautiful daughter. Obviously, it could be misinterpreted. It didn't justify the unhealthiness of people, but I almost understood them.

We moved from the group to various game tables and walked along the soccer, softball, and basketball courts. We were more than seven hundred employees, and I now understood why this meeting was being held in a place like this. People were having a great time. I walked with Jimena along the hacienda facilities, watched a game, and ate and drank something from the intermediate stalls.

In the afternoon, after lunch, which we shared in an indoor hall, I changed, and when I went out to the large outdoor hall, an orchestra was already playing the first notes of dance songs. As soon as Alicia saw me, she approached me.

-You missed out, my love. You've spent the whole day with the mousey girl. Don't say later that you weren't warned,- she said without any more words. She came close to almost touching me to be able to talk to me over the volume of the music. She was wearing a revealing white miniskirt dress with very high cocuiza heels. Despite being over thirty, she was an attractive and eye-catching woman. Every time she walked;all eyes followed her. I didn't know how to end this offensive move without risking something about Jimena's secret, but I had to get out of this ambush before she appeared, which could be any moment.

-You should know, Alicia, that everyone hangs themselves where they want. With your experience, that should be your knowledge.

-What do you mean? You don't mind being second fiddle?

-Second, third, fourth, if you find pleasure and feel good, you can't criticize someone for using their free will, right?

-No sir, yours is truly pathetic, you make me feel embarrassed for you.- She looked at me with fury and walked away swaying her hips with each step, drawing more attention to her legs, her backside, and the low-cut dress that I had not noticed before. I watched her as she walked away and suddenly felt the heat of Jimena's gaze on my left cheek. I didn't need to process it; I knew it was her eyes burning into me. I sighed and slowly turned around, knowing what I would find.

There was her fury. She had seen me watching as Alicia walked away, but she probably didn't see what had caused her to storm off like that

Jimena approached slowly, wearing an all-red outfit that emphasized her skin and hair color. The dress hugged her body until the hips and then flared out into bell-bottoms, giving her an elegant look. She had a belt that matched her high-heeled camel-colored shoes, a silver choker, and a thick bracelet of the same color. I had no words to describe her, she looked spectacular with her body, beauty, and touch of elegance.

-Don't look at me like that, I saw you appreciating her...- She didn't finish her sentence.

-My beautiful love, how dare you think that? You didn't see the first part, I was just watching her leave, and yes, I was surprised by how much cleavage she was showing, but you should have heard what she said to me and what I said back, and why she stormed off in a fury. I don't think she'll bother me anymore, or you.

-Well, I don't care, if you like her.- I laughed loudly, drowning out the music.

-I don't like her, the only one I like is you, and I can prove it right now if you let me kiss you in front of everyone.

-We can't do that, focus, you haven't told me anything.

-You told me not to lookat you like that, but that look was saying that I have no words for...

-No, that look was guilty.- She interrupted me. -That I caught you with your Alicia, but you still haven't told me anything.

-If you let me bite you, it's better than all the words I could say. You're beautiful, you outshine the entire party, you're the most beautiful one here.- She smiled, and her demeanor changed. Her anger towards Alicia dissipated.

Jimena was a striking woman, but she was also a girl when it came to love. Fate had been cruel to her at such a young age when she was supposed to be spreading her wings in society, with friends, at parties, and in relationships with men. It truncated the experiences that she was supposed to have as a teenager and later as a woman. She had to work to help her mother make ends meet, complete her studies at night, and excel in everything she did. Achieving academic success while working and having only the hours of noon, midnight, and weekends to live limited her ability to experience life to the fullest.

During the party, when the dancing started and the tables were set, José sat with us. Jimena told him everything about me. She told him the truth - that we liked each other, that we were going to start a relationship, and that I knew everything about her.

He took it very well. At first, he objected, saying that we had very little time getting to know each other, but we both told him at the same time that we were going to take it slow, and he calmed down. He asked me to respect her, to consider her, and to treat her like a hidden treasure. He gave us a lot of advice on how to maintain a relationship and build a home from the beginning while we were young. He offered his support for whatever we needed,and we agreed to figure out how to handle our surnames and ties. I was moved by how much he loved her. I could see that even though her father was not there, José played that role with profound affection.

We talked for a long time, and at first, people looked at us without missing a detail. But after Jimena and I danced a couple of pieces and returned to the table to keep talking with him, the interest disappeared. We danced, had dinner, and enjoyed the night. When the party ended, we made our way back together, first by bus and then by taxi. Nobody was surprised to see us together anymore.

I left her on her porch, and we finally kissed again. I had been longing for it all day. It was hard to say goodbye; I could not find a way to let her go, but it was late. Her mom noticed that she was outside, and the next day we started what would be a new life for both of us. In my case, I had to start my professional job with the team I had been assigned to, and I had a girlfriend that I could not even have imagined in my wildest dreams. And she started a journey where she was no longer so alone; she had me to support her and keep her company.

The speed at which my life had changed since that June 17th at 7:45 am surprised me. It was not just that I found a job at one of the best law firms in the city and the country, or that the economic conditions were unimaginable for me and compensated for the deficiencies we had been going through at home. It was that, in addition to all of that, I found Jimena.

I had never felt for a woman what she inspired in me. It was daring to call it love when it was just beginning. It would have been irrational and immature to say that I was madly in love. It would have been irresponsible to see it that way, but I could not find the word or feeling to describe it.

I was also feeling a wake-up call of an extrasensory connection that I did not want to acknowledge at first because my scientific mind told me that these were things from books of superstitions and old family members. But when I thought of her, vivid images of her house, her body, her thoughts came to me as if I shared them with her. I felt sensations that I had never experienced before.

On July 1st, I started my professional work, and I had to work hard to keep up with the different cases assigned to me and the associates I worked with. Despite all of them being very good and kind people, they were also excellent professionals and therefore extremely demanding and jealous of their work. I could participate in cases with two or three associates at the same time, in the same number of cases, and none of them understood that I was working with the others. Therefore, they wanted almost an exclusivity of our time for their cases.

It was not personal. In occasional conversations with the other assistants who started with me, whom I saw very little, they told me the same thing. The pressure was immense, and we had to be committed and focused to avoid making mistakes. Any distraction could cause a case to be lost or the least damage could be that we would have to incur more time and loss of fees for the law firm, which could be catastrophic for the progress of our career.

The intensity of the work and Jimena's routine made it so that we saw each other very little. We talked through chat, but in a limited way because she almost always had the associates on top of her to finish the work on time. To see her more often, I decided to always arrive at 7:30 a.m., go up to the 42nd floor, and wait for her for 5 or 10 minutes, kiss her secretly, smell her, touch her, feel her, and talk very quickly. At noon, we only chatted when she was not too busy studying, and sometimes I would pick her up at the university to accompany her home.

This was going to be her last semester, and her graduation would be in December. She wanted to maintain her grades and devoted all the time she could to studying. On Sundays, we usually went to the movies, and sometimes I tried to find her on Saturday night, but she was very tired and preferred to sleep.

It was in that routine that we established that one night we were saying goodbye on the porch and the door of the house opened and Jimena's mom, Mrs. Mila, came out.

-Good evening, Mr. Adrián, how are you?- she said very kindly, a Jimena with 20 or 25 years more and a few extra pounds. My face must have been one of total astonishment because I remained silent longer than necessary and they both burst out laughing.

-Good evening, Doña Mila, how are you? Nice to meet you, excuse me...

-I didn't know you were stuttering,- Jimena said, unable to contain her laughter. -Surely you hadn't seen my mom, didn't you know she looks just like me?

-No, you never told me, I couldn't imagine it, and I haven't seen a photo of you two, but I always asked you to introduce me to her, didn't I?- I didn't know what to say or how to justify myself.

-No, she's lying. You didn't want to come in, I was begging you to meet her.

-Jimena, for God's sake...

-Don't listen to her, she's always teasing like this. If you play along, she won't stop. But come on in, don't stay out there any longer. From now on, you can drop her off here in her house.

That ishow I started going to her house on Saturdays to have dinner and share with her mom. The three of us would come up with anything to share, watch movies, play Monopoly, tell family stories, which turned out to have many common places, like maybe the stories of many families.

One Saturday, I took her to meet my friends, among them were two female friends with whom I had relationships, nothing serious, just things from adolescence and youth, but nothing that went unnoticed by Jimena. She detected them right away and put them under surveillance. In general, everyone was impressed by her beauty and her gentle yet lively and insightful demeanor, which demonstrated her superior intelligence.

With time, I also realized her emotional intelligence. She handled most situations with tact, patience, and discretion. When she told me to relax and that something didn't affect me, in relation to a work situation, at first, I thought it was a feigned indifference to avoid facing the facts, but knowing her well, I realized that most problems didn't actually affect her. She wisely chose the moment and way to handle them so that they did not influence her mood and daily life.

That iswhat the warnings she gave me about other women were also about. They weren't jealousy, but rather a reminder that shenoticed, and we were under her watchful eye.

Then it was her turn to meet my family. My mom made her favorite pasta, baked macaroni, and we shared the whole night. Jimena charmed them to the point where they all ignored me, and she was the center of attention. She enamored them much faster and deeper than she had done with me. They accepted her immediately and my parents considered her a daughter from that same day. After that dinner, I had to hide or avoid the topic because they asked me too much when I would propose to her and when the wedding would be.

Another Saturday, we went dancing with the same group of my friends. It was our first night out drinking and dancing, and it was almost the end of September. The weather had changed quite a bit, and the cold that precedes the winter season was felt.

When I went to pick her up at her house, she was wearing a long black overcoat, very elegant, down to below her knees. She had it closed up to her neck and looked like a European woman ready to walk the streets of Paris. I greeted her, kissed her, and told her how beautiful she looked dressed that way. We got into the taxi and went straight to the disco where the group was waiting for us. When we entered the venue, she left her coat with the receptionist.

When she finished taking it off, my jaw dropped as if the ligaments had disappeared from my face. She was wearing a gold leather miniskirt with a beige blouse and black high-heeled booties. The skirt covered what was necessary to say that she was dressed, and her long and impressive legs, which I have already talked about, seemed to have no end, and forced one to look for the spot where they met.

I spent the whole night uncomfortable, not because of how she was dressed, but because I was thinking about how to undress her completely. She must have suspected because she looked very comfortable sneaking glances at me and smiling. I imagine she had caused the desired impact because she was happy. It was the perfect night, we had a great time, and the detail of dressing like she had never seen before brought up the inevitable conversation that we had both postponed.

We made the journey back to her house in complete silence, holding hands in the taxi. My friends had contributed a lot to that silence.

As we said goodbye outside the club, the comments about how Jimena looked continued to turn into jokes and insinuations that it was still early and we should end the night well, that breakfast was included, that we should be careful not to get pregnant toosoon, a ton of usual jokes that, although not a taboo subject for us, we had not discussed. In my case, I had been delaying it.

When we got out of the taxi, I walked with her to the porch, we kissed each other goodbye, we had barely spoken. I took her hand, we stood at the front door of her house, and we sat on the windowsill next to each other.

-It's late and it's cold, Adrian,- she said very softly.

-Yes, but we need to talk. Do you want to talk about it?

-Yes.

-I don't know about your experience in this, I haven't asked you, and I'm not going to ask you now,- I started to speak slowly and choosing my words carefully. I had clear ideas, but I hadn't rehearsed how to communicate them to her. However, like almost all our issues since we met, it seemed like they were pre-discussed. She knew what I wanted to talk about, and there wasn't much introduction needed. In this case, it was the same, from the beginning, she already knew what I was referring to.

-None,- she replied almost instantly.

-I told you I wasn't going to ask you...

-None,- she said to me again without letting me finish. She looked down and I thought I saw her blush; I don't know if it was from the cold or the confession. I took both of her hands to warm them up and to reaffirm the contact of the skin that already existed between us. I leaned in towards her face and spoke to her, almost touching her cheeks.

-Okay, none. Then my intuition worked perfectly,- I nodded, -it wasn't a topic for us to discuss or bring up in these first few months that have passed, but I won't say that I haven't thought about it every minute, every second that I've been with you, since the first day I saw you.- She separated her face slightly, smiled, and shook her head in disapproval. -Okay, let's say not every second, but maybe every five seconds, something indeterminate, but it's always been on my mind and in every part of my body. Do you want me to explain what I'm thinking?

-Of course I do, I want to know what's on your mind, but please don't say anything suggestive,- I smiled and shook my head this time. -Women,- I exclaimed.

-Okay. Look, it's not easy everything that I've been thinking and feeling. I've thought about it a lot because you mean a lot to me. In a short time, I've fallen in love with you. In a very short time, I feel like I know you well. The connection we share makes it so that many times I know when you go to bed, when you wake up, when you're not in the building, or whether you did well on an exam or not. When I check the clock, it's because it's time to write to you or to pick you up from university. I've become so used to those telepathic messages that I fully trust them to plan my days.

-You know that I feel the same way about you, in the same way.

-I know, you've told me. Maybe I haven't told you like this before. It's most likely that you have a broadcasting antenna in your body and I'm just picking up those signals. Well, wanting to preserve our relationship at the highest level of pure feelings, I've been putting off the topic of consummating that love. But to achieve one thing, the other is necessary. To maintain the depth and purity of love, its realization is necessary. One cannot exist without the other. Platonic love is doomed to extinction or memory if that love is not put into practice in the only way that a man and a woman can love each other.- She interrupted me and kissed me.

-At the same time,- I continued after the long kiss, -there is a very powerful opposing force, which is that sexual energy is the most devastating force that humans can emit. It can build and elevate a relationship to unimaginable heights, but it can also sink it into the lowest passions and destroy what we thought was that elevated love. That has been the dilemma I have been carrying all these months. I didn't want to propose or insinuate anything to you because I wanted you and me to be sure of what we wanted. We could have had a more casual relationship based on the physical, and we would have already made love,- she shook her head and squeezed my hands.

-That's not what I want with you. It's not why we met.

-Exactly, that's not what I want with you either. In these months, we have built that great and elevated love. We have gotten to know each other, and we trust each other.

-Do you want to ask me if I'm ready to make love with you?

-I don't want to ask you that. I wanted to hint at it, make it more subtle, but it seems like you're cold and want to go to sleep,- she laughed loudly, and we both turned to see if it had any effect on waking up her mother.

-No, I don't want to go. Yes, I'm cold, but like you, I've been thinking about this. I didn't want it to happen if we weren't sure, and I'm sure that you're the man I want in my life, now and forever,- the way she said it, innocent and candid, touched me.

-That's the only way a relationship should be accepted when a man loves the woman only because she is his woman, and the woman loves the man only because she wants him to be her man.

-I understand. So, it's our case.

-It's our case,- I lifted her and kissed her for a long time before she went inside her house. She was trembling the whole time while I kissed her. I think I was also trembling, feeling her so close and being able to discover her curves through the thick coat made my skin tingle.

The following week was a hectic one. She entered the midterm exams of the semester, and I finished two cases I was assigned to.

We saw each other very little, and we never touched on the topic again, but you could feel the tension on both sides in the preparations. I had been thinking about the place, the moment, how to get her out of her house for enough time, creating an atmosphere so that it would be something beautiful and unforgettable. Every time I saw her, I noticed she was nervous, and every time I hugged or pulled her by the waist to kiss her, I felt the same trembling from last Saturday night.

We agreed to meet on Friday night, I would pick her up from the university and accompany her home, and we would probably have dinner with her mom. She messaged me on the chat app telling me not to pick her up from the university because she had gone straight home, and that if I wanted to see her, I could come over later after dinner. I thought it was a good change of plans, as it was out of the routine. I asked if her mom would join us and if I should bring a bottle of wine for the evening, and she replied yes, her mom would be glad to join us.

I left my house around 9:30 pm, I had changed into my latest pair of jeans, a fashionable t-shirt, and white sneakers that looked brand new. I bought a French Bordeaux wine that was a bit pricey, but I thought the different evening was worth it.

I arrived just after 10 pm. She had told me to come in as the door would be unlocked. I followed her instructions and when I entered, the house was dimly lit, with no sign of Jimena or Mrs. Mila. I sat on the couch holding the bottle, and everything seemedvery strange to me. I called out softly so as not to appear rude but received no response. I was getting more intrigued by the minute, so I got up just as Jimena appeared from her room.

She was wearing a bright blue silk robe that reached her knees. It had a thick border and was tied with a belt of the same color that fell to one side of her hip. The robe made her pale white skin stand out too much, and her light brown wavy hair cascadeddown the sides of her chest like a waterfall of golden curls. Again, as always when she impressed me, I was speechless and stunned.

-Aren't you going to say anything?- she asked, standing in front of me with one leg forward, making the robe open up halfway. I still couldn't speak.

- Where is your mom? I stuttered.

- Where is your mom? Is that all you're going to tell me? Should I turn around and change?

- Don't even think about it - I said, almost shouting, and then she started laughing with her usual mocking tone, and then a little nervous.

I approached her and hugged her, kissed her slowly at first and then with all the passion that I had been holding back for months for the most beautiful, sweet, and at the same time explosive and sexy woman I had ever met. I continued kissing her on the cheeks, neck, smelled her hair, her nape, kissed her chin, her eyes, her entire face.

I loosened the knot of her robe and let it roll down her shoulders, it fell to the floor behind her, she had nothing underneath the robe. I continued kissing her from top to bottom, lifted her up and we entered her room. There are no words to describe what that moment meant for both of us, it cannot be narrated how the greatest and most sublime thing that a couple can do reaches its peak beyond pleasure and pain, beyond imagination and desire, as when two people complete the union of their cravings for flesh and satisfaction is shared between accomplice kisses and caresses of what happened.

- Are you going to tell me where your mom is?

We laughed non-stop, left the room, had a glass of wine, and went back to bed, repeating it until the bottle was finished. Our bodies had fit together perfectly. It seemed like we had been long-time lovers, everything was synchronized between us, the tasteand desire to take from one another what the other gave you were expressed in the same rhythm.

I stayed the night and left around mid-morning on Saturday. At breakfast, she explained that her mom had gone to spend Friday and Saturday on a farm with a friend and would arrive at night. I went to pick her up again in the afternoon and we went to the movies.

That's how my relationship with Jimena began, the real relationship, we didn't have fights or important differences, time went by with us going to the movies less, seeing our friends less, and sharing less with our families. We had given ourselves to each other and every free moment we had was dedicated to being together.

What did increase was our spiritual connection, I couldn't call it anything else. Whenever one of us intensely thought about the other, we would write or call, and the message was always the same.

I was thinking about you so strongly, I want to see you or be with you, I need you by my side, I miss not seeing you today. I thought about consulting someone, but I did not know who, and whoever I told had the risk of raising suspicions of insanity or being seen as one of those people who hear voices.

In December, Jimena's graduation took place. After the ceremony at the university, her mother prepared a small gathering with the family, which was not very numerous, only José Ariztimuño, his wife, and their young son, a cousin of Jimena's mother, my parents, my sister, and a few friends.

She graduated with the highest honors, and that same day, José gave her the news that she would be accepted into the law firm as Jimena Ariztimuño Llovera, taking her father's surname, and as an exception to the firm's rules because she was the niece and only daughter of the deceased twin brother of the main partner, they would take her as if she were José's daughter.

We were all very happy, she was going from one emotion to another, she was radiant. Mrs. Mila and José approached me to talk about how well the relationship with me had done her, how she had changed, and how the sadness that I saw in her at the law firm anniversary party had dissipated. They showed me love and gratitude for making their daughter happy.

When everyone left, I stayed to help them clean up the house. After we finished, we went outside and sat on some wicker chairs they had in the backyard, and Jimena sat on top of me.

-Thank you for everything,- she said.

-I don't understand, thank you for what?

-I don't know, I just feel like thanking you. You have given me so much these past few months that it seems like I am a different person.

-Did you guys' plan this or something?

-What? Who are you talking about and what are you talking about?

-It's just that your mom and Jose caught me earlier - I realized it, she told me - uh-huh, and then they told me the same thing, thank you for this and that, that I've made you happy, and so on. She smiled, but this time I saw the sadness again. That was when I understood.

-We didn't plan this, I haven't talked to either of them about this.

-My love, my dear love, I understand what you're going through, I understand that you wish your father were here, but I don't want to sound cliché, but I'm sure he's watching you somewhere and must be very proud of you. Besides, if you don't believe he can be around us, what is certain is that he is inside you, you have his blood and you are the best representation of all the good he must have been. You can't come to this world and bring a woman like you and not be someone special.

-You see why I thank you,- she kissed me gently and slowly until I felt tears running down her face. I held her tightly in my arms and responded to the kiss with the greatest love and the greatest tenderness I was capable of.

-Today I felt several times the same thing I felt that day when I was in class and they called me that my dad was in the hospital, a strange restlessness, a premonition reaching me, a fear that grips me and I don't know where it comes from.

-My love don't be afraid, that's already over.

-Yes, but I don't want it to happen again, I don't want to lose another loved one, I don't want to lose you.

-You're not going to lose me, there's no reason why you would lose me, I'm never going to leave you.

-Hug me, hold me tight, don't ever leave me, not you.

-Jimena, my life, don't be afraid, fear darkens love, envelops it in darkness and deprives you of enjoying it, these months we have given ourselves and we have reached our love, don't let anything obscure it. I'm not going to leave you for anything.

-Yes, I won't be afraid. We're together and we're going to stay that way.

Several days passed before Jimena returned to her normal self, it was difficult for her to return to normalcy, the graduation ceremony where a proud father was supposed to be present for his daughter's achievementscould not happen, she knew it and I didn't realize how much it hurt her to keep moving towards that goal.

I was only able to see it when the day had already arrived. I have always regretted not seeing it coming. We celebrated Christmas, New Year's, and returned to work. She continued as Jose's assistant, she had to wait until mid-June to join the assistant training course with the new recruits that year.

In February, during the coldest part of the season, we went to the movies and returned early to her house. Her mom was not there, which surprised her quite a bit. She called her and her mom answered saying that she would spend the night playing cards with a friend. So, in addition to the movie, we had the house to ourselves, which we did not expect. We made love with an unusual softness, touching and feeling each other slowly, with deep and heartfelt caresses. We went from a slow and deliberate intensity to an imagined lightness.

We remained quiet, enjoying what we had just done, without comments, breathing in love and skin at the same time. I do notknow why I didn't stay overnight, maybe it was because we didn't know what time Mrs. Mila would come back, but it always seemed strange to me when I remembered this moment, why I said goodbye and went home.

I took a taxi and got off a few blocks before my house. I passed by the bar where my friends were probably hanging out, but that was not the reason I got off there. I did not understand why I looked at them through the window and didn't go in. I had no intentions of going in, I just watched them for a while and continued slowly on foot to my house. I went in and strangely found my mom and dad awake, drinking beer and listening to music, just like in the old days. I hugged them tightly, asked for their blessings and went to bed. I did not see my sister, there were no clues that she was nearby.

At first, it was difficult for me to fall asleep, but when I finally did, I fell into a deep, heavy sleep from which I tried to wake up and could not. I thought I was dreaming on several levels, like a movie I had seen with Jimena. Jimena, I remembered her. I felt distant from her, as if I had known her a long time ago, as if what I knew about her was because someone had told me, like a story about someone close to you whom you have not seen in a long time and whom no one mentions anymore.

But no, it wasn't that.Jimena was my girlfriend, the woman I was in love with, with whom I had reached the gates of heaven more than just making love. I felt trapped in this dream, I should have stayed with my dad and mom talking to them and drinking beer, or at least with my friends at the bar, but falling into this dream from which I can't wake up and feeling a drowsiness that invites me to sleep deeper I don't like it, it's like going down another level, how many more will I fall before I climb them and wake up.

Jimena gave me a goodbye kiss at the door, she told me I could stay but that I was risking Mila taking away the blanket and finding us, we just laughed at the thought, anyway, I went in. Had I returned?

I saw her lying in her bed, next to her on a chair was the indigo blue robe that inspired my desires so much, I felt the blood burning inside me and desired her like a madman, as if I had never possessed her, I approached and lifted the blanket that covered her, she didn't wake up, she was curled up with her hands in her lap sleeping on her left side, so I climbed onto the bed and hugged her from behind, I wanted to feel her warmth, I passed my right arm over her body but didn't find it. I was in my bed alone without a blanket and I felt very cold.

I made the decision to wake up, I could not keep going with this dream, I had to go up, but suddenly everything became clear, I heard Jimena's voice calling me and I followed the voice. Gradually I was able to regain my senses, it was as if I had taken a sleeping pill, as if the food from the nighthad something that drugged me, I came back to my senses and then I felt myself waking up, when I opened my eyes there was Jimena, she was looking at me with concern, but when she saw me wake up her face changed and although she was crying she looked happy.

-I thought you had left, you told me you were not going to leave me, that you wouldn't.- I sat up on the bed and hugged her.

-My love, I told you and I will keep my promise, I am not going anywhere, no one will ever separate us.- She sat on the edge of the bed, allowing me to embrace her tightly. Finally, we were together again. I closed my eyes and breathed in her scent, kissed her neck, grabbed her hair, and ended up kissing her on the lips. I felt her naked skin under the navy-blue robe.

I jumped up, fully awake. I could not believe it. How long had that dream lasted? I still felt the heaviness of deep sleep. I got up, went to the bathroom, and washed up. I became fully aware, and my heart was beating fast. Jimena, I thought. I got dressed quickly; it was too early for it to be Saturday. It was not even 7:00 a.m. yet. I was not going to call her because she would be asleep. I decided to head over there. I had a feeling that would not go away, and I didn't want to go back to bed. I looked atthe bed, and fear made my hair stand on end. I practically ran out of the house. Of course, everyone was still sleeping in my house. I remember my parents were partying the night before.

I took a taxi at the corner and headed to Jimena's house. I did not know what excuse to give for arriving so early, but I would figure something out.

When I got out of the car, I felt that something was wrong. I ran to the porch and saw the door to the house slightly ajar. I ran inside and to Jimena's room. The sheets were tousled, and on the chair next to the bed was the navy-blue robe. I searched the entire house, and there was no sign of either of them. I called Jimena more than a dozen times, but shedid not answer. I called Mrs. Mila, and she answered on the third call.

-Come to the Hospital, Adrian.

I felt my life stand still. I saw everything happening in slow motion. When I arrived at the hospital, I did not know where to go. I asked several nurses, and one told me to go to the intensive care unit. I ran up the stairs, two or three at a time. When I arrived, there was no one to ask. I called Mrs. Mila, but she did not answer anymore. I went down to the morgue, but no one was there. I went back to look for the nurse who gave me instructions, but she had already left the hospital. I closed my eyes and took a deep breath. I heard Jimena's voice calling me and followed her.

I crossed the street in front of the hospital, and I could still hear her. She led me to a park. In the deepest part of the park, there was a small forest, and under the most lush bush, surrounded by white and pink hibiscus flowers, was a bench. Jimena was sitting there, waiting for me.

-My love, here you are. I was so scared, I thought something had happened to you. Don't ever scare me like that again. You know I can't live without you. I hadn't told you before, but it's true,- I said. I saw that sadness in the depths of her coffee-colored eyes again, but this time it was unavoidable, much bigger, as if sculpted in her soul and visible through a window.

-You don't have to be scared. You told me yourself that fear was overshadowing our love. There's no more fear. We won't be afraid ever again. I'll always be with you,- I sat beside her and hugged her. The coldness that came from the fear of what could have happened to her faded away as I felt her warmth and the steam that our love produced in the open air.

FIFTH STORY

THE STARS

Astronomers have no doubt that 97% of our body is made up of stardust. This means that we don't need to search for extraterrestrial life, because we are it. I imagine that some people have a little more and others a little less, but on average that is what we are: bodies made of distant stars.

If that is the case, then we have visited unimaginable places in the universe, in our solar system, and have been part of other bodies such as rocks and comets. We have traveled millions and millions of kilometers, only to end up gathered on a remote planet in the outer rings of a small galaxy called the Milky Way.

When we turn to dust, the winds, tornadoes, and hurricanes will lift our remains back up towards the stars, and we will continue the interstellar journey that temporarily placed us on Earth. Or maybe we'll mix with someone else's remains from this same planet and a bit of another galaxy, and then we'll feel like we're a little bit from here and a little bit from there.

As these ideas came to my mind and I tried to figure out where I came from and where I would end up, one idea in particular caught my attention: how did I end up here on this planet, how was I born exactly where I was born, and how did I end up living the life I've lived? To express that thought, I wrote this verse:

How many stars are in the universe,
how did I end up here in this one,
how did I meet you
and why did I fall in love.

*****

My name is Nadine Giraldo, I was born in Buenos Aires 22 years ago, and I am the youngest of five siblings. The three eldest are boys and then there are two girls. We all have a three-year age difference, so my natural playmate was my older sister. My contact with my brothers was very scarce. When I opened my eyes to the world, I was around 4 years old, and Jorge, the third of my siblings, was already 10 and had no interest in playing or socializing with a shy and spoiled little girl.

The two oldest were already in high school. The three boys went to the military, graduated, and were assigned to border posts in the Pampas, and my older sister studied to become a teacher and is always very busy with planning and tasks. We were a group of numerous siblings who did not take advantage of being together when we were little, and now we see each other very little. Life takes everyone down the path they have to follow to fulfill their destiny.

Now, at 22 years old, I graduated in psychology with honors, and the University offered me a position as an assistant professor. I accepted immediately. At this age, I had not thought about where or what I would be working on after finishing my studies, and it is very simple for me to start teaching what I have loved for the last 5 years. The problem is that the position is not for the School of Psychology, but for the Faculty of Engineering.

They want me to serve as an assistant professor for some social subjects that are taught as electives in that faculty. It is hard to believe that exactly what I had always done, avoiding the environment of engineering, mathematics, calculations, and consequently, the people who like that science and who are naturally opposed to my personality, would present itself as my first job opportunity, and one that I really liked. I had no other choice but to accept the teaching job at that faculty, even though it is not my environment and the premonition that lit up in my chest when I signed the contract with the Dean.

I do not want to be misunderstood; I studied psychology because I was sure it was what I liked, and I confirmed it with the diligence with which I learned every book, the grades I got, and the comments of the teachers and classmates. However, I still feel very young, and I am afraid of what my first experience as a professor might be, especially in an environment very different from the one I had become accustomed to in recent years.

As I said before, I had shied away from exact sciences because I believe my brain thinks differently. I tend to turn many ideas over in my mind at the same time, and each idea generates another set of problems or solutions. I like to review and meditate on them thoroughly. Those who know me believe that I am naturally quiet, but when they let me speak, they can't find a way to make me stop. I explain everything that I am thinking, I examine every aspect of each thing and I describe the various scenarios that each one can led to.

Engineers are not like that. They want concrete, fast, and precise solutions. I do not think that way. I am a bit more convoluted, and I find it hard to see things in a simple and straightforward way. I think that is why I liked the degree I studied from the beginning.

I thought about it carefully and decided to accept. I interviewed with the head of the humanities department at the Faculty of Engineering. I wanted to teach the class -Study and Understanding of Man- to students in the common cycle. That means everyone who chose to study engineering, regardless of their specialization, would be in my class. It was a huge task for my first assignment, having to deal with newcomers who are more concerned about their calculus, math, physics, and chemistry classes than a humanistic class, and me trying to teach them about the genesis of personality, affectivity, psychoanalysis, human behavior... Oh God, what have I gotten myself into?

If you have imagined a little about how I am, you may have already deduced that I have not been very successful in the boyfriend section.

Setting aside modesty, which is not very useful at the moment to convey what I want, I have to admit that I am part of the group of beautiful women, and why not say it, I have a good body. I am not exuberant, but I am thin, have a good bust, and an acceptable behind.

So, it was not for a lack of physical attributes; on the contrary, when those attributes began to appear, I hid them. I wore loose blouses, wide-leg pants, knee-length skirts, and no makeup.

Despite all that, men always approached me like flies, which caused me many problems with the other women around me. Since I never showed much interest in almost any of them, the problem only got worse.

Those who experience this will understand me perfectly. So where does that leave me? I'm attractive without trying to be, I'm popular because of my way of expressing myself, without trying to be, and at the same time, I'm shy. Yes, a disaster.

I had only one boyfriend from the age of 16 to 20, and since then, I have not had any other relationship. What happened with Alan? Very simple, he became too possessive. He said things like, you are getting too beautiful, I was the first, and now you are mine. I made the mistake of giving in to him when I was 19, and wedid not last for more than 10 months after that. I focused on finishing my degree, studied like crazy to achieve the goal of graduating with honors, and forgot that men existed. I would havetime later to think about that.

It seems like the moment has arrived, because ever since I signed the contract to start teaching classes and was given the subject I would be teaching at the University, the idea began to form in my mind that I was becoming the exception among all the women I knew and those I didn't know as well, because having 22 years, a good body, a good face, a job, and nobody to look at you, to accompany you, to write to you, or to call you, is sad.

The social pressure around me had started since I broke up with Alan, my mom, my sister, my aunts, the few friends I had, and even my dad, who had always been jealous, hinted that if I continued to be so apathetic with relationships, I would end up very abne. The phrases did not wait: -You do not go out much, that's why you don't meet anyone,- -You are too independent and scare men away!-, -Why do not you dress up a bit more? You arealways dressed casually,- -And you... when will you find someone?-

Well, it was about time, and I started to get ready for my first day of class. I woke up very early, I had not left any clothes out and I knew it was going to be difficult to dress up trying to change my look at the last minute. I showered and went to the closet to find something to wear. I tried on all the skirts, and they were long, old-fashioned, and outdated. No wonder Idid not have a boyfriend! I tried on the pants, and it was the same, the blouses were even worse. My eyes were watery, it seems that the prudish girl wanted to let loose.

I had not thought of any of this until Sunday night and despite it being early, I was starting to panic. What could I wear that would not make me look like -Annie the Orphan-? I went to my sister's room and borrowed a skirt and a blouse. I put themon, and it was not so bad. The skirt was a little above the knee, not too short, a soft orange color, and the white blouse matched perfectly. I was going to have to go to a mall to buy something, not too much because my savings were notvery large, but something for sure. I let my hair down which I always had in a ponytail, put on some makeup, and left.

On the way to the University, I thought it was all very strange, how I was feeling and thinking about a relationship when I was going to meet first and second-semester students whose ages shouldn't exceed 20 at most. Although I am 22, a person of 20 is a child to me. I am one of those women who prefer a relationship with an older man, not too old, of course, but older than me and, above all, mature. Yes, because there are 30 and 40-year-old children who never grew up.

I registered at the door, took the list of students, and headed to the classroom, carrying all the planning I had done during the previous week before the start of classes. When I entered, the room was half-full, but the list said it was a full classroom. Ten minutes were left until the start time, so I sat and waited. At 7:00 a.m., I closed the classroom door and cleared my throat so that those who were still talking could hear that the class was about to begin. I was acting, copying the roles of the teachers who had taught me and whose style I liked the most.

The majority sat down and gradually fell silent as I began to speak to them. At first, some looked at me incredulously, others with doubt, and I could see some mocking and insolent glances. Nothing I didn't expect.

Some stragglers continued to enter, not disguising the same looks in the same three categories. I started talking to them and did an icebreaker to get to know each other and introduce ourselves. I explained what the class consisted of and what the evaluation method would be. As a result of the unchanged looks, I decided to toughen up the experience a bit and told them how strict I was going to be without caring about their other classes. The atmosphere changed completely, the mocking and incredulous looks ceased, and a small murmur of disapproval began to grow. Nothing I didn't expect.

Then something unexpected happened, the last straggler entered, stopped next to my desk as if asking for permission to continue, and we stared at each other without speaking. He lowered his gaze and slowly raised it, scanning my entire body, almost undressing me. I felt like even my underwear, which was the nicest I had, wasn't staying on top of me. That thought completely betrayed me, and I felt flustered. A shiver ran down my back, and my stomach rose and fell suddenly, thankfully, because it made me react.

-You may come in but let this be the last time because you're interrupting the class,- I said. I felt myself blushing, and he noticed. -Sure, sorry, teacher. I couldn't find a place to park my car,- he replied with a very mischievous smile. He was a man in his mid-twenties. What was a man doing in my class? I didn't expect it. -Well, you're not here to serve me. You're here to study and to be on time,- I tried to sound as stern as possible, but my voice betrayed me. I wasn't fully recovered from the undressing this guy gave me, and I couldn't play along with being called a teacher.

-Oh, but sorry if you've already lost it before the class even started. No problem,- and what I had been avoiding happened. The whole class burst out laughing. I closed my eyes, turned red, slowly turned towards them, and made absolute silence. My face must have been terrifying because they suddenly stopped laughing, and the laughter was cut off like with a knife. Moments of tension followed, and it was either them or me.

-I remained very serious and tried to fix what that guy did to me in terms of the class's trust, and especially what I felt when he looked at me.

-Mr. Herrera is already going to sit down and let us continue until we finish the class, and ten minutes before the end, he will give us a summary of everything we've covered today,- I challenged him. I couldn't let myself be intimidated, and I couldn't lose authority in front of the rest of the students. But I was wrong. He passed very close to me and whispered, -Nice skirt.- I remembered my underwear again and blushed once more. I pretended nothing had happened and continued with the class, not looking at him anymore. With 10 minutes left to finish, I reminded him that he had to give a summary. He got up and came calmly to my side, very close.

-Can I give the summary here, right? No problem,- he said, looking at me.

-Of course,- I replied. I regretted it again. He stood next to me, almost brushing my shoulder, and began to summarize the class. He said everything, as I had explained it, even the first part before he arrived. I don't know how he did it; I think he asked someone who recorded me or a student with a very good memory. While he was summarizing, I moved slowly to the side so that his presence wouldn't affect me, but he followed my movement slowly, as if he didn't want to. When he finished, I gestured for the class to leave and went to pick up my things. He followed me.

-Look, ma'am, I want to apologize,- he began, but I interrupted him.

-Look, Mr. Herrera, stop the game because I won't allow you to disrespect me from the first day,- he interrupted me.

-No, no, don't misunderstand me. Really, it's just that I've never stopped calling female teachers 'seño,' but you're the only one who has been bothered. I'm sorry, please,- he sounded very sincere, and it seemed that I was the one overreacting to the term 'maestra de niños.'

-Okay, let's leave it at that, but you can't use 'tú' with me.-

-Why not?

-Because I am the teacher, and when a teacher uses 'tú' with a student, they lose the trust of the other classmates. Can you understand that?- My voice was losing its tone and sounded furious.

Truthfully, no, I understand why you have to address an old-fashioned and outdated professor, but for you, who are the most beautiful teacher I've had in my 100-year career, I don't have to use the formal -usted- - I tried to completely ignore the last phrase. She spoke to me softly and slowly, not stopping from looking me up and down.

-You can't do that either, you can't start a class by complimenting the teacher. If they hear you, you can be expelled from the University, it's not ethical.- I couldn't find a way to defend myself. -And you're still using the informal 'tú.' - She looked me up and down again, stopped at my legs, slowly scanned them, looked at them as if she could see through my skirt, stopped at my chest, and stared into my eyes.

-Alright, from now on I will address you as Professor Giraldo.

-And stop looking at me like that.- Those words slipped out of my mouth, and now I truly regretted them.

-What? No, no, no, no, how am I looking at you? How can you forbid me from looking at you, from talking to you, from looking at you? Should I just drop the class altogether? I don't think it's ethical for a teacher to limit a student like that.

-You're still using the informal 'tú.'- It was the only thing that came to my mind.

-No, I said 'profesora.'

-Everything else...

-What about my gaze?

-Nothing.

-Something happened, because you're bothered.

-You're still using the informal 'tú.'

-What about my gaze, will you tell me or not?

-Nothing's wrong with your gaze.

-But you said something.

I quickly gathered my things in the middle of our conversation or the game he had established between us. I wanted to run back home, crawl into my bed and cry. I felt like this first day had been terrible only because of this guy whowould notlet me be myself, who had me disoriented and out of control.

-I already told you Herrera that nothing was happening, that you can go and that you must keep your distance- - I regained my composure and felt that I was getting back on track, but I hadn't finished speaking when the folders I was picking up fell to the floor, the sheets came out and scattered around the desk, the other students had already finished leaving and only the two of us were left in the classroom.

-But look what you've done, for not wanting to run away and not answer me- I bent down to pick up the folders and sheets and looked at him angrily from the floor.

-Can you help me pick them up, Mr. Herrera? since as you say, this is your fault.

-Ooh, finally we understand each other, yes, it was because of trying to run away and avoid my -look- that bothers you- - he was pushing me to the edge, few times had a man managed to do that to me, but I couldn't find a way to make him leave, stop talking to me and not look at me anymore. Something suddenly made me understand that maybe I didn't want him to leave, but to keep doing what he was doing.

-Are you going to help me?

-Are you addressing me informally?-I had no choice but to laugh, I couldn't keep fighting anymore.

-Well, well, when you laugh, you're more beautiful, sorry Professor Giraldo, but that slipped out- he crouched down next to me and I felt his gaze between my legs, tightly pressed together, it was very fleeting, but I'm sure of what I saw. I spoke hurriedly trying to conceal my agitation and squeezing my legs tighter so nothing could be seen.

-I don't know what to do with you, I mean with you, you confuse me, let's finish picking up and leave, okay?- - I took control again, at least that's what I felt.

-That's fine with me, where are we going?- it's unbelievable how quickly he can make me lose control.

-Nowhere - I almost shouted - I'm not going anywhere with you, can you understand that?

-I'm just repeating what you said, let's finish picking up and go, I'll go anywhere with you,- at that moment a professor with a physics and math look came in, we had already finished picking up.

-Good morning students, would you be so kind as to lend me this classroom for the next class?- I was going to answer that I wasn't a student.

-Of course, Professor Zabala, as you wish, we're done here and on our way to grab something at the cafeteria, right Nadine?- he replied shamelessly. I didn't want to talk anymore because I was very angry and there would be time to see the professor again and introduce myself properly. I looked at him angrily and twisted my eyes, letting him lead me by the arm towards the door, his hand on my skin was burning me, when we went out I pulled my arm away, almost dropping the folders again.

-Ok, Mr. Herrera, if you don't start respecting me, I'll have to report it to the school,- I started.

-Nadine, I don't see why we can't talk like two normal human beings outside the classroom and stop acting like the old and senile teacher you're not.

-What do you want?- I replied.

-To talk normally, like two people our age, I'm 25 and you're what, 26, 27?

-Twenty what? No way, I don't have all those years.

-Oh no! And let's see, how old is the teacher?

-Since when do I have to answer to a stranger or rather a newly known student how old his teacher is? That seems like a lack of respect to me,- We continued walking through the halls of the faculty until we reached the parking lot, obviously he was the one with the car -Well, this is where I get off, I'll take public transportation. See you in the next class.

-But Nadine, didn't we agree to go somewhere?- He kept addressing me informally.

-No, really, we didn't agree on anything, we were just walking, you asking anything.

-And you not answering anything, but if you want we can go to a cafe and have breakfast?

-No, I don't think so, I have to go home and prepare the next class - I tried to lower the tone to a neutral one and not of discussion to say goodbye as what we were, teacher and student.

-But it's just a 10-minute walk to Puerto Madero, we can have breakfast or just have a coffee and you can tell me about the class, then I can take you home, I have nothing else to do today.

-You're really persistent, aren't you? No, it can't be done.

-Tell me, why can't it be done? What's wrong with having a coffee, two people who have just met and are going to share a class for a semester? I don't see anything wrong with that. Also, agree on how we're going to talk, you call me -tú- or -usted.

-Agree with yourself first, which question do you want me to answer?

-That's easier, let's go eat something, have a coffee and discuss all this, doesn't that seem simpler to you than staying here where everyone is watching us, the teachers, the students, the university staff, I mean everyone, is that what you want to avoid?

-That's it.

-Well, it doesn't suit you very well then that they see us, here, look, let's go through that side and nobody will see us - He was referring to a side exit from the parking lot that had a covered hallway. I agreed to avoid continuing with the scene of tug-of-war with a student on the first day of class, the truth is that it didn't suit me for another teacher or a school executive to see me arguing in an unprofessional manner with a student.

-And where are we going? - I asked when we had already left.

-First, let me help you with those folders, they don't look heavy but they're all disordered and if they fall again, they can get damaged - I tried to refuse his offer, the question was rhetorical because I had no intention of going anywhere with him, but I liked the gesture, it seemed very kind, in these times when there are hardly any gentlemen left, I handed him the folders and we continued talking and walking very slowly, as if without a destination, towards anywhere.

-How did you change so much? University affects you, inside you were almost a jerk, unfriendly, and now you're a handsome guy.

-It's not that I changed, it's you who changed. I'm still the same unfriendly jerk. Who told you I changed?- I burst out laughing, I had made a mistake.

-Sorry, it wasn't my intention. I'm not usually hurtful to people. I guess you made me feel uncomfortable in class, and that made me want to get back at you.

-Well, well, the psychologist at her best. That was a very quick self-psychanalysis, wasn't it? - His tone had changed; he was speaking sweetly and condescendingly.

-Don't mock me, don't make me regret apologizing. I'm saying sorry, and you're making fun of me.

-I'm not making fun of you. I just love seeing you in action as a psychologist. Besides being a good teacher, you must be a good professional. Have you ever thought of doing clinical psychology too?

-I have thought about it, but one thing at a time. I'm finishing my studies, they offered me this teaching position, and I need to consolidate myself here at the university before seeking other paths. - I was surprised by the question and answered honestly and openly. Something was changing in the way we talked. - But enough about me, don't you think? How is it that you're 50 years old and in your first semester?- I asked, and he immediately burst out laughing.

-I'm not 50, I'm 25, as I told you. But it is weird, isn't it? - He kept laughing - What happened is that I finished one degree, and I want to study another. Since the degree I finished didn't include some electives like -Study and Understanding of Man,- the department administrators made me enroll in this class this morning. Simple.- I was left with my mouth open for a while. Everything I had assumed and thought about Fabricio wasn't true. I had to start over and try to decipher who this guy really was. He looked at me with a certain mockery, and I reacted.

-Sorry, I didn't mean to...

-How many times are you going to apologize today?- he said, dead of laughter - It's okay. I noticed from the look you gave me when I walked in that you were imagining all sorts of things about me, so I thought I'd tease you a little. So, I'm the one who owes you an apology. - He made a bow with the folders in his hands. I threw a punch into the air as if reproaching him for everything he had put me through.

-So you're a psychologist too, then. I don't know what degree you studied, but it seems to have something to do with human behavior since you knew what I was thinking and all. Accepted apology.

-No, it wasn't psychology. It was -Study and Understanding of Women,- which they made me repeat. That's why I'm in your class.

-Very funny, but surely you must have a few women waiting in line for you - I don't know how I could say such a barbarity, I regretted it immediately. Of course, he laughed louder than he had all day.- How long are you going to laugh at your teacher?

-I'm not laughing at you, but at how much we've progressed in such a short time. I had forgotten about you being a teacher until you just mentioned it, haven't you?

-Well, actually no. You have to tell me how you knew what I thought of you, and while you're at it, you haven't told me what you think I thought.

-That's precisely why I didn't pass the subject and have to repeat it. I can't handle a tangle like that, a woman confuses me more than galaxies.- And now we both laughed.

-It's very simple, if you want me to explain it to you. You have no way of knowing what I thought, unless you tell me now that you can read minds and have extrasensory powers, so I would recommend a healer and not a psychologist. You're making up things to make me feel bad and keep apologizing to you.- I tried to tangle up the concepts so that he wouldn't realize that I had guessed exactly what I had misinterpreted about him.

-If you apologize, it's because I'm right. That part I can unravel very easily, in my slow brain to argue with a woman. And besides, it's already clear that you shouldn't keep believing that I am what I am not.

-Oh no, that's not it. You're really annoying. You tried to make fun of me in front of the other students on my first day of class.

-Well, what a ton of information you just gave me.

We had walked along Avenida Independencia towards Puerto Madero for about ten minutes, slowly talking. We entered the first cafe we found, which belongs to the chain of American cafes that are everywhere. We left behind the large and luxurious office buildings, the headquarters of banks and multinational companies, to enter the bridges and warehouses of the port, now transformed into a tourist and gourmet attraction of the city.

The marine environment and the lagoons in front of the port changed our mood and the conversation became less tense, more relaxed, and a little more intimate despite the short time we had known each other. At first, while we were walking, we sometimes brushed against each other because of the discomfort of passing by people who were walking either faster or in the opposite direction on the same sidewalk, but as we were getting closer, the contact became common. Three, four steps, and a light touch on the shoulders, legs, arms, it was a synchronized and pleasant movement that seemed like camaraderie, which became a necessity. All of this happened in 10 to 15 minutes.

-Yes, it's fine, but please don't use it against me.

-Not at all, just don't go telling everyone that it's your first-time teaching, and that today was your first day and that you got nervous with the first idiot who came into your classroom late.

-Well, calling him an idiot is correct, I don't understand why you have to behave like that, if being yourself is nicer.- I tucked my limbs back in, blushed, and he noticed and burst out laughing.

-Thanks, but no teacher had called me nice until the third or fourth class, it's progress, don't you think?- he said, winking at me.

-Well, if you want to make fun of me a little, I might turn around and go back to the University, what job do I have?

-Well, no, I don't want to, I'm getting used to it, give me some time to adapt to your rules and I promise not to...

-It's not my rules or that you make fun of me,- I interrupted. -It's just that, you know, a little respect for your teacher.

-Okay, more respect, agreed, but stop talking about leaving already,- he said. We entered the café, took a table outside, which seemed better to enjoy the good weather and the scenery. Fabricio went to order at the counter, a coffee for me and a breakfast with coffee for him. When he returned, we continued chatting as I said before, calmer and more intimate.

-So, are you going to tell me what you studied before registering in Engineering?

-Yes, of course, it's no secret, I'm not a government spy or anything like that, but promise me you won't laugh.

-Oh, I know, don't tell me. If you think I'm going to laugh, it's because you were a circus clown, because you don't need to study for that,- he looked at me seriously.

-See, you've already started, and I haven't even told you yet.

-I promise not to laugh,- and I burst out laughing.

-Well, I studied nothing less than Astronomy. At the illustrious University of La Plata, at the Faculty of Astronomical and Geophysical Sciences,- I couldn't help but laugh, I laughed like crazy for minutes. I looked at him and laughed again, his face went from serious to annoyed.

-No, no, no, excuse me. It's not that I'm laughing at the career, but at how boastful you sounded when you were saying every word from the degree, the university, the faculty, hahaha, no, no, no,- I stopped laughing and he kept looking at me, serious and angry. In the end, his face changed and he burst out laughing even louder than me. I couldn't help myself and we both laughed until we almost cried.

-Let's stop now, really your profession doesn't make me laugh, on the contrary, I think it's a beautiful career. I didn't even know that there was such a career here in Buenos Aires and that astronomers were trained in the country. So, tell me, what do astronomers do in Argentina?

-Nothing. That's the problem, there aren't many astronomers, but there aren't many jobs for us either. I chose that career for other reasons, I studied it because I'm fascinated by the stars, galaxies, and the formation of the universe, more in an existential and poetic way than in a scientific way.

-Wow, that sounded deep. I'm sorry for laughing, it wasn't my intention to make fun of your profession.

-No, forget it, it's silly. I know why you laughed, I myself tried to make you laugh because you're much more beautiful when you do, and today I haven't been very good with you, I owed it to you.

-No, you didn't owe me anything, it was me who magnified the whole situation with my first-time teacher nerves, but look, here we are talking about the best, tell me, why did you study Astronomy? a minute ago you said it was more for poetry and philosophy than for science, how is that?

-Well, I have to make a living, right? And as I told you, astronomers don't have much job opportunities in the country. If I want to work in that field, I would have to go somewhere else. So my father wasn't very happy with that, and he and my older brother have a small construction company that has given us a more or less good living. So if I want to get into the business, I have to study Civil Engineering. That's all.

-I understand, that's very reasonable, you're not going to be able to build buildings on the moon, Mars, or the sun - I laughed again.

-You already apologized, stop it because the next time I don't think I'll forgive you. Is that part of your revenge, right?

-Of course, you made me suffer a lot in the classroom and part of the way here, besides you're going to keep apologizing- I said with a little bit of coquetry - but that doesn't answer my question, you said you studied that career for other reasons.

-You're looking at me like that again and I swear I forget that you're a teacher of a mandatory subject I have to take, and my world and yours will crumble - I laughed again, unsure if it was with coquetry, nervousness, or wishing he would keep his promise.

-You're doing it again - he said.

-Okay, I'll calm down and stop looking at you because I just discovered a ton of information about how easy you are - and this time he laughed - but are you going to tell me or not?

-Okay, I'll tell you. To start, I'd have to go back to when I was a kid, but that puts me at risk of you wanting to charge me for the psychoanalysis later - I shook my head as a sign of no - okay, if you're not going to charge me, then it's easier.

-As I told you, -he continued- when I was little, I wanted to be a poet, I wanted to be a writer, and I started writing when I was twelve or thirteen years old, but sometime later I realized I wasn't that good and suddenly stopped writing. Then I moved on to the next phase, which was reading, and I became so fond of reading that I read everything, from the newspaper to any book or magazine that fell into my hands. I started to take a liking to philosophy and history books, and I realized that in the past, there were advanced knowledge of all kinds that were lost between wars, invasions, migrations, and especially in the Middle Ages, when most of the world's population was forbidden to read books that contrasted with religious knowledge, including astronomy knowledge.

-Very deep, -I said very softly and convinced of what I was saying. It seemed to me that while he was talking, my concept of his person changed completely- but go on.

-Well, the more I read, the more logical it seemed to me to study a career related to what I liked, and I really liked stars and everything related to the origin of life, not so much in its biological form and evolution here on Earth, but rather from the true origin, which is the beginning of everything, the moment when nothing exploded: -The Big Bang-. That's why I studied Astronomy.

-Impressive, you know that I'm even a little envious, healthy envy, but it's envy. You did something that very few people achieve and do, which is to study what really fascinates them, what moves them inside. And tell me, what did you achieve, where did that career take you? Did you find what you were looking for?

-What do you want me to say? It's like any career, there are subjects that exceed your expectations and others that don't. You think they don't leave you anything, like what's the point of this in my entire future life until the day I die.

-Like the Study and Understanding of Man?

-You know, no. I don't think your subject is one of those, I think there is a lot of good material in understanding human behavior - I was still impressed, he didn't seem like the same person from a few hours ago.

-And did you achieve what you were looking for?

-In a way, yes. It's incredible how similar in concept what I imagined when I was trying to write poems is to the reality of life and the stars.

-Oh no, but tell me, because I'm getting curious, I don't know what you mean - I smiled at him, very interested in knowing what he was telling me.

-It's like your smile, like how we went from repelling each other a few hours ago to being attracted and interested in each other, that's how the stars and all the universe's celestial bodies behave, so similarly.

-No, no, no, don't come with that, there is no attraction or interest here, don't exaggerate.

-Well, there is, I have it and I'm not afraid to say it, you have it, but you're a woman and what a woman - and he looked me up and down, taking in everything visible while I sat in the chair - and then you don't want to admit it, but there is - he said it with complete conviction - I didn't know what to answer.

-Okay, let's suppose you're right, there is an interest in me, but it's nothing more than wanting to know your complete story, see, that's the interest - I winked at him and smiled.

-That's the interest, and attraction is something else, is that what you mean?

-If I don't say yes, you're not going to finish the story, right?

-Difficult.

-Okay, interest and attraction, a lot of attraction - I said, laughing.

-You know you feel attraction, a person like you doesn't lie - he said it, and internally I knew he was right, very right, but I wasn't going to tell him or admit it, an hour after meeting him, he continued - I learned many things, besides the scientific ones of course, I learned or confirmed what I always suspected, that we all in this Universe come from the same thing, that sounds a bit religious maybe, but it isn't, we are all one thing and I can agree with those who promote the Unity theory, they say itspiritually, I can say it scientifically, we are One, there is nothing or no one separated from the other, there are no different kingdoms, animal, vegetable, mineral, etc. however you want to call them, there is only One and that was created billions of years ago with the big explosion, the Big Bang.

-That no longer sounds like a scientific career, it sounds like understanding and comprehension of life, how did you get to all of that?

-It's very easy, when two beings like you and me look at each other and are attracted to each other - he comes back to that, I looked at him and definitely looked at him flirtatiously, he had earned it - it's because the material they are made of is compatible, the material they are made of attracts, it calls out, and it seems to be something incomprehensible, and we call it from the heart, love at first sight and many other things, but it's just simple, it's just that the material we are made of is compatible and it's meant to be together.

-Wait a moment, you're confusing me. Are you taking away the romance from two people falling in love at first sight?

-No, not at all. On the contrary, I'm saying that the love that we feel is a result of the compatibility of the material we are made of.

-I see. Could you elaborate on that? Which material are you referring to?

-Don't you understand? And here I thought I was speaking very clearly. Sorry, sometimes I assume things are understood. The material I'm talking about is simple, it's stardust, that's what we're all made of. Each and every one of us, no matter which kingdom we belong to.

-Wow, that's actually more romantic,- I applauded and almost melted in my seat, staring at him in awe. -And how are we made of stardust?

-You must come from the most beautiful, grand, and fabulous star in the Universe,- he said, and I melted even more, inviting him to continue. -Well, at least I discovered that the claim that we're made of stardust isn't original to me or even a poet. It comes from an American scientist who said it and it went viral like 40 years ago. It's simple and true and has to do with the formation of the Universe, stars, planets, and everything that exists.

-Can you explain it to me?

Please translate the following paragraph from Spanish to English, strictly adhering to what is written, please do not include anything of your creation:

-Well, we have to start by knowing that the primary material of the Universe is not rocks or minerals as we know them, it is Hydrogen and Helium, that's what the Universe was made of.

-And how did we come about?

-The celestial bodies that formed after the -Big Bang- concentrated Hydrogen and Helium. These celestial bodies transform, and the Hydrogen runs out. This process takes billions of years. Then it synthesizes into Helium and Beryllium, and the process continues.

That's when we say the star is dying. Depending on its size, the star can either turn into a white dwarf or a red giant. The latter, when it dies in its process, forms iron. When the iron disintegrates due to the immense gravity at the center of the red star, it implodes and creates a supernova, which is nothing more than an explosion. But since it encompasses many materials, much size, and many light-years, we compare it to celestial bodies. In reality, what this supernova has done is create material for new stars, new planets, what we know as asteroids, comets, and especially stardust. That stardust travels billions of light-years through space, creating places and connecting galaxies, carrying traces of life from one place to another. That's where we come from, that's where everything around us comes from, that's where the certainty that we are one thing comes from. Imagine, if a supernova can do that, what the Universe did when it exploded a very, very long time ago, creating each of the stars, galaxies, constellations, and living beings like us made of flesh and bone, or beings that are very different, made of light or energy, and who knows what other material on other planets or very distant stars, beings that can be very different from what we are here on Earth, but that undoubtedly are part of us because they come from the same place and the same thing that formed everything on the first day, the first instant the Universe saw the light.

-Wow - I couldn't believe it - Did you come up with all of that yourself?

-Unfortunately not, if I had said it first, we wouldn't both be sitting here - he smiled and looked at me, maybe with the same look I was giving him, it was a moment that lingered and in which I felt we connected, he lowered his gaze, his head and continued - what I can add to that is that the attraction between two people has its explanation in the material they are made of, starting from the fact that on this planet there is all the necessary matter to make life and that's where we come from, from the genetic material of our ancestors, it is also true that for billions of years before we knew life as we know it today, Earth received dust from the stars in large quantities that was integrated into that DNA we have, in fact we keep receiving it, day after day we are bombarded by that stardust and energy from the farthest reaches of the Universe, I have no idea if anyone has been able to determine how much of those emanations from outer space mixes with human beings, but my theory is that the more celestial matter we share with someone, the chemistry that brings them closer, enamors them, makes them live next to each other and need each other to share a life together, the more compatible they will be and the more attraction there will be.

-That's very beautiful what you're saying, it resonates with me a lot because I studied the mind and behavior of human beings, and within behavior is the will to love, the need to feel loved as one of the basic needs for human beings to live a fulfilling life. Now, you're saying that depends on the stardust we're made of. What about someone who has stardust from a unique star and doesn't have a compatible partner? In other words, someone who is alone here?

-No, remember that's not possible, we are One. We all have something that is shared with others, we come from the same place, and not only do you have the luck of being able to find someone who loves you and whom you can love because you share the dust of the stars, but also because coming from the same place, you can and should love all your fellow beings, because by loving them, you are loving yourself because they are the same thing, the Unity.

-You're right, it's even more beautiful if you look at it that way.

-Even more beautiful is feeling like you're entering a class you didn't think you had to take, arriving late because you weren't registered on time, and when you cross the door, you see a stunning woman in an orange skirt who makes your life smaller and makes you remember all your crazy theories of the stars and cosmic dust that now seem like magical dust, fairy dust. That's more beautiful - now I lowered my head, we entered into a territory that I never imagined I would reach with someone in such a short time.

-Fabricio...

-Nadine...

-Listen to me, please - I started with a very quiet voice, not knowing what I was going to say after each word - you know that I am your teacher, you are no longer a child whom I teach, as a teacher I cannot have anything with a student, and even talking like this right now, it's not right, I never thought that coming to have coffee with you here would end up like this. We had a good time, we talked well, but it's not good for what I want to do...- he interrupted me, and I thanked God, I didn't know how to continue, all the sentences I said sounded empty and cliché, nothing of what I truly felt or thought.

-Nadine, I already told you what I think and feel, save the speech of the new teacher in the new position, it's okay, it's the first day I met you, it's true and I don't want you to lose the opportunity to be the teacher (or the seño) for anything in the world because of me - we laughed - you're right, it's not fair and it's not ethical, but I'm not asking you to be my girlfriend today, of course not, what I'm asking is that you let me be close to you, that you let me conquer you, that you don't see me just as a friend or as a student, I assure you that I will respect the exact time of the semester, I won't ask you for anything that isn't just to talk to you and be in your life, not as your boyfriend, for now, but as that shadow that you need, that follows you and doesn't disturb you but that you get used to and miss afterwards - I looked at him deeply and felt that he was right, there is something different when you meet someone whom you had not known before but you feel completely comfortable with and know that you can trust, and I decided to trust.

You're right, nothing I said before is true. The truth is that I like you more than I should,and I don't see anything wrong with what you're suggesting as long as you respect my boundaries and don't cross the line in the classroom - no calling me -seño,- no making my life difficult, no looking under my skirt, and no other disrespect.

- I agree with almost everything, except for the part about "looking under my skirt".

- What do you mean?

- That I didn't look under your skirt.

- Yes, you did. Of course, you did. Do you think I'm blind?

- I tried, but I didn't see anything. You wouldn't let me.

- Shameless and he admits it. No, no, no.

We continued talking almost all morning. At noon, we walked back to the university parking lot. At one point while we were walking, he took my hand for a few seconds. I let go because I did not want anyone from the university to see us holding hands. But in that brief moment, I saw something that plunged me into a stupor, from which I snapped out of when he almost shook me.

I saw myself as an old woman holding an urn containing someone's ashes and pouring them into the sea from a bridge, which could have been one of these bridges in Puerto Madero. When I searched within myself to know whose ashes they were, I realized that they were Fabricio's, and that he and I had had a long life together with children, grandchildren, problems, and happiness, but in the end, a life full of love. When I came back to my senses, he asked me:

- What happened? You went into a trance or something?

- I don't know. I time-traveled like a hundred years, I don't know how many. I had an inexplicable vision. It's the first time something like this has happened to me. - I didn't want to tell him that I saw us together for a lifetime. It was premature.

- Can you tell me about it?

- No, it was something very strange. Maybe someday I'll tell you, but it was from the future. I don't understand anything.

- It's easy to understand. Did you know that time travel is theoretically possible?

- No, I don't know anything about that. Another one of your celestial theories?

- Well, the most famous of all, the -Theory of Relativity,- isn't mine, by the way. Do you know that we live in a world that most people consider three-dimensional, right?

- Well, yes.

-Well, no, the truth is that Einstein postulated, and later it was proven, that our universe has four dimensions. To the three known ones, you have to add time, and when you do that, time becomes relative too, especially when you reach the speed of light.

-And when do you reach the speed of light?

-This one is mine, with thought. Scientists measure the speed of thought as the responses to brain interactions, but what about imagination? How long does it take for you to imagine yourself on Saturn or even farther, in the center of the galaxy? In those moments when we use the power of thought, we can reach speeds greater than the speed of light, and when we do that, we can travel through time and reach the heights of perfection, clairvoyance, and transformation. We go beyond the unimaginable and become transmuting matter of knowledge. A good meditation can transport us to places that do not exist in the physical world but in other dimensions. So, whatever you saw could have been a small trip to the future that your mind, detached from the constraints of the physical body, achieved through the projection of the speed of your thought into the dimension of life expected in the planet's movement.

-Do you think so? Maybe it was that. One day we will know, and thanks for that theory, you surprise me more every moment.

When we arrived at the Faculty, I took the bus to go home. Idid not want him to drive me. It was better to take things slowly. If we were going to have several months to get to know each other before starting a relationship, it was better to go slowly. According to his first theory, we had traveled from very far away at unimaginable speeds to land on this blue planet. Who knows, billions of years after we arrived, we met and can share our journey together and someday return to being stardust, as in my visbn.

SIXTH STORY

ABSENT

Day to day never ceases to surprise us, we can be with someone for a long time and may not know them, not know their deepest and most intimate desires and aspirations.

When we lose contact with a loved one that we assume is feeling and thinking the same as we do, surprises can arise that catch us off guard and trigger crises that disrupt the course of our lives.

Meditating on the situations that can lead us to this, is why I wrote this verse:

At what point did I not realize,
when did you stop loving me?
When did I start to notice that you no longer looked me in the eyes?
When your kisses only felt on the lips?
Why is there no warmth in the sheets anymore?
And now what do I do with all of this?

*****

Isabella Rosas was born in a small town on the northern coast of Colombia in the Department of Antioquia. Her parents had moved to Montería when she was very young, and she had grown up in that livestock city, but she constantly visited Arboletes to swim at the beach. She loved being able to go to that town and forget about everything. Isabella was what every young woman from the coast represented and more cheerful, talkative, relaxed, and witty, with an exuberant skin color that was not quite white nor dark but transmitted all the exotic beauty of the Colombian woman. She had long black hair and a tall, slim, and very stylized figure.

Isabella arrived in Medellin in the midst of what she would later call a series of wrong decisions. She had just won a scholarship to study architecture at a university with a campus in the city where she grew up. However, the scholarship was awarded to the capital of the Department in which she was born, so it seemed appropriate for her to move to her native Department to continue her studies. Moving alone to Medellin had to be a good adventure at her recently turned 19 years old.

Roberto Mendy had finished his architecture degree two years ago. He was the son of one of the most famous architects in the city, with the same name, a very prolific builder in both Medellin and Bogota who had started, along with other colleagues, the trend of using red bricks in both cities.

Roberto Mendy Senior, Roberto's father, was the son of another builder with the same name, a French immigrant who had arrived in the city at the beginning of the 20th century and dedicated himself to building all types of constructions throughout Medellin. He made sure that his only child in Colombia studied architecture and dedicated himself to the same profession, so the name already had three generations and was widely recognized. Roberto Mendy Senior had been widowed when Roberto was very young and decided not to remarry, so he had no more children, leaving the last of the generation as the heir to the company and many other properties.

Roberto was not like his father who had died the previous year. At the age of 25, he found himself with a construction company, an architecture firm, and other investments in both companies and real estate that his father had managed intensively and had grown year after year. Since he was old enough and found himself alone in the house with the tutors his father had used to complete his education, he always thought that his father's frenzied pace was due to loneliness and missing his mother.

He had already decided that he did not want to live that way, and when the decision came, he did not hesitate. He closed the construction company, reduced the activity of the architecture firm, left the investments in stocks as participation, and handed over the real estate investments to a manager who would only return the rentals. With everything the restructuring of the inherited properties brought him, he would live the rest of his days in peace. He could dedicate himself to having a wife, children, and a well-cared for home.

In his well-planned life, the way he met Isabelladid not seem right to him, although he never mentioned it to anyone, let alone her.

He had applied to be a professor of Architecture at the Pontifical Bolivarian University, with the recommendations and fame that the Mendys had, it was impossible not to get the position. He planned to teach what he learned at the university and what he saw in the field alongside his father for many years. In addition, through the architecture firm, he could complete two or three lucrative projects per year that would supplement his inheritance income, a sufficient workload to be able to focus on his personal plan.

Isabella had settled in the city and had started her first semester in college. She had already been there for three months, and the change was very hard for her. She was used to the landscapes of the plains of

Montería, the mountains, the hills, the weather, and the people, everything was different in Medellín. The vivacity she had, and her way of speaking didn't seem to please everyone. She was starting to have a crisis when some classmates invited her to dance. That was what she liked, that was the environment she had come to this bigger city for, to have fun.

She did not hesitate for a moment and put on her shortest dress and highest heels, she did her makeup, and when her friends saw her, they were impressed. She looked like a model, a beauty pageant contestant, they said. -Well, let the Paisas get used to it because that is how thewoodswallowof Montería are- You're not from Montería,- they replied, -you're Paisa too.

-Ah yes, alright, but from the coast, where everything is more delicious,- and she showed them her cleavage. They all laughed and left.

The group of friends was quite large, but Isabella noticed a guy who looked foreign. She asked one of her friends about him and she replied, -Wow, you have an eye for the best. Girls from Monteria come sharp, haha.-

-Why? Tell me, friend, don't hold back.

-He's a little French guy whose dad left him a mountain of money as big as Medellin, everything, dear.

-Hmm, interesting,- Isabella replied.

Roberto had gone out to celebrate being accepted as a professor at the university. He accompanied a friend who had invited him, saying that new girls were joining that semester. On the one hand, he had to celebrate, but on the other hand, he felt a bit uncomfortable because he was so young and had to think about respecting the female students in the faculty.

But oh well, it would only be for tonight, and he hadn't started teaching yet. When he saw the tall, dark-skinned girl in the short dress, he felt something different. His usually cool French blood was stirred in a way he had never felt before. It wasn't her clothing that caught his attention, but her figure, her manners, her audacity, her laughter, and her boldness. She looked him in the eyes, and he approached her. They talked and danced all night.

They left together, and he took her to his home, an apartment in the Sabaneta area that his grandfather had built. The small apartment had been rented by her father with great effort to provide her with more security, at least so she wouldn't have to pay for tuition with the scholarship she had earned. The drinks they had consumed led to him staying the night. Isabella didn't think much of what she had done; it was the first night, they had just met, and she had given in. For her, having three months alonein the city, it seemed too fast.

Roberto continued searching for her for the next 15 consecutive days, he was enchanted, he had never been with a woman like herbefore, there were none in his social circle and there weren't many like her in the entire city. However, everything had been so easy with her that something made him uncomfortable. He loved her, that much he was sure, but maybe he would have preferred things to happen differently.

When he started teaching classes, he had to prepare material for several weeks, including projects and models, so he thought it was the appropriate time to take a step back and think better about what had happened with Isabella. He stopped looking for her for a couple of days and thendid notcall her again for a week.

Isabella noticed the change in him. At first, it seemed very normal to be with someone who was totally opposite to her: quiet, formal, serious, and above all very rich, a millionaire. But after a few days, she thought that their personalities were not compatible and that a long-term relationship might not be the best for both of them. So, when he began to distance himself, it seemed comfortable and convenient to her, and she did not seek or pressure him.

When Roberto received the call from Isabella, he was missing her, longing for her. Nights with her were passionate and different, her company made something of the passivity and natural tranquility that had characterized him since childhood wake up, and he could feel the sensation of vibrating that he could not achieve with other people or his normal activities. That is why he was content to hear her talking on the other end of the phone. He was not expecting the call, and these were the things that bewildered him about this woman. Shouldn't he have been the one to take the first step to look for her?

-Hello Roberto, how are you? I hope very well,- she said, but her tone sounded strange. -I don't want to bother you, I know you're very busy, I'm busy too, the semester is tight and I'm behind on several things, but excuse me again, I would like us to see each other.- This time, she sounded a bit solemn.

-Sure, I'll come to your apartment tonight, is that okay?

-No, I prefer we meet somewhere else.

-Okay, where do you want to meet?

-At the mall, this afternoon at 6:00 p.m. I'll treat you to a coffee, okay?

-Perfect, see you there,- he replied, intrigued. He continued working and did not think about the call anymore.

Isabella had been thinking about calling him for more than a week. Despite her young age, she was a woman with clear ideas and concepts, and calling a man who does not seek you was not part of her tactics. Moreover, she had her own doubts about what she felt for him.

It was true that she liked him. The fact that he represented the opposite of what she was seemed like a safeguard to avoid any deviation from her personality, like the one she had with Roberto the first day she met him. That is why he would serve as a fortress for her weaknesses. But at the same time, she had doubts about whether she could survive so much seriousness and formality. She had to talk to him to dispel the doubts and come to an agreement.

-I'm pregnant,- she said as soon as he sat in the chair across from her in the cafe.

Roberto stumbled over the tablecloth, spilled the water they had brought while she waited, and almost fell to the ground. When he got up, he looked at her face and burst out laughing.

-Isabella, for God's sake, can't you see that you almost killed me? Another one of your jokes.

She looked at him and burst out laughing too, almost crying. Suddenly, the laughter disappeared from her face, and she said, -No, I'm serious.

An endless silence fell between them. Neither knew what to say, and neither wanted to be the first to speak. They stared into each other's eyes as if trying to guess what each was thinking and what the correct next action between them should be.

Roberto lowered his eyes. He thought that all his life he had wanted to have a family. That was what he had planned. He had thought of meeting a beautiful woman who would represent him in society and make him proud. He wanted to have children to give them the home he never had, the present and dedicated father he never had, and the mother he never had. And now, suddenly, a woman he hardly knew but fascinated him was telling him that she was expecting a child from him.

Isabella was thinking of getting up and leaving. She had not thought about how to tell Roberto she was pregnant, and the way she did it seems like it was not the best. If there was a chance for them to come to an agreement, it seems to have vanished. She stared at him, trying to guess what was going through the handsome man's frozen face, transported to another place. Surely, he wanted to be somewhere else, to run away and leave her alone with her problem.

Despite her young age, she was willing to take on that child alone. At first, she thought she would never tell him. But as the days went by, she recognized that a father had the right to know that he would have a child, so she invited him to meet. But to launch the news abruptly like that was a very bad strategy. He lowered his gaze and could not maintain eye contact.

Roberto raised his eyes and saw Isabella making a gesture as if to get up. He did not realize how much time had passed without looking at her. He took her by the arm and told her to stay.

-Let's talk, what you just told me is very big, excuse me for being stunned, but a child is the greatest thing that can happen to a person - I had already made a decision, destiny has very strange ways of making you reach where you plan to go, time is not a very important variable either, what is important is knowing how to identify the right moment of when you have to take what life puts within your reach.

And just as everything in Roberto's life had come effortlessly, a child also came, so why should he object to the way it came? This was his child and Isabella was from a good family, in his opinion, middle-class, but from a good family. She was not a womanof society, but she was very intelligent. She was in Medellin thanks to a scholarship she won at the University and knew how to handle herself very well. Moreover, with the figure she had, her beauty and liveliness, she would have no problem adapting to his circle of friends and life in the city.

-Sorry for the way I told you, yes, it seemed like a very bad joke, but it's true. What can I say, I'm not asking you to take care of the child and me, I know you haven't called me in days and I understand everything, but I thought it was only fair that you knew you're going to be a father. You yourself told me your story, the death of your mother when you were very young and your father's recent death, so I didn't want to leave you without knowing that you won't be so alone anymore.- Everything she said was from the heart, she couldn't have been more sincere.

-No, forgive me, if I stayed silent it was because you surprised me, I could expect anything but this news.- Roberto was moved to hear her speak in that way, he could identify her sincerity and was deeply moved. It was true that he was alone, he had no relatives and was the last of the Mendy'sdynasty. Having a child and a woman to take care of and form a home with came unexpectedly, but it was what he wanted. He took her hand and gently said:

-Isabella Rosas, I would never, listen to me well, never let the mother of my child be left alone to raise and see him grow. It's something you and I are going to share, we're going to do it together, neither you nor I are going to be alone, we're going to be accompanied by that child and each other, and if God allows it, more children will come.

-What are you saying Roberto? That you're going to take care of me because I'm pregnant? That's not the woman I am, that's not why I called you and that's not why I told you this.- She spoke again very sincerely, raising her tone and looking upset. -That Isabella Rosas you're talking about came to this city to pursue a career, to study and to uphold my family's name. This pregnancy doesn't change my plans at all, and I already told you that I know very well that you didn't call me because you didn't want tocontinue, but this happened and I had to tell you.- She stopped talking because tears welled up in her throat like a torrent, and she couldn't continue.

-I haven't said anything about that, please calm down, let me explain. If I didn't call you, it's because, as you know, I got accepted to the university and I have to prepare classes for the whole semester, give classes, and present them to the coordinator for approval. I've been working until midnight every day, giving classes and then going back home to keep working - he tried to sound as convincing as possible, partially it was true - now you know what we went through during the days we were together, it was no coincidence that you got pregnant, you know how much I like you and everything we talked about when we were together, I haven't told anyone else, you are the only woman I have been intimate with in this way, so it's not forced for me to be with you, on the contrary.

-Okay, and how do you plan to take care of us as you said?- She was listening carefully and looking at him fixedly in the eyes, trying to find a clue if what he was saying was what he really felt, but she couldn't see any disparity between the two.

Roberto hadn't thought about that, it was true that hehad made the internal decision not to contradict Isabella with the assertion that it was his son, it was also true that he had decided to take care of both of them, but the most important decision was still missing.

-Marry me,- he said.

This time it was Isabella who burst out laughing and almost knocked everything off the table, he went too far, she thought. The least she could expect was that suddenly, without discussing it properly, without meditating, without thinking, Roberto Mendy, the richest young man in the city, would propose marriage to her, she was carrying his child, but she was only 19 years old and had a life to live. Getting married was not her immediate goal, nor was having a child, but that was already irreversible, but marriage, for God's sake!

-It's serious, to repeat a phrase I already heard today.

-I know,- she replied, -I accept,- and even she was surprised.

The wedding took place three months later, Isabella did not show any signs of pregnancy and was able to wear a wedding dress like she never dreamed of. The reception was held at the Country Club, and in addition to her mother, two cousins came to Medellín to help with all the preparations, given the number of guests. Roberto's guests were all from the high society of the city, while Isabella's guests were all from her family.

Before getting married, Roberto had already taken her to live in the Mendys' house, a mansion of over 800 square meters on a plot of 2,000 square meters in Los Balsos, in the El Poblado area. It was built by his grandfather, renovated by his father, and he was working on plans for its remodeling when Isabella arrived at the house.

They had a son, Roberto Junior, the fourth generation Mendy. The pregnancy months passed very normally,and time flew by. Roberto had adapted to the idea of being married, and Isabella didn't have much time to think, between the tasks of marriage, preparing the baby's room, contributing her own ideas for the remodeling of the house, and establishing herself as the new Mrs. Mendy in Medellin society, everything was happening very fast.

Roberto ran up the stairs as he always did after finishing his daily training. He opened the door to the room and saw Isabella sitting in front of the dresser, with her torso uncovered and sitting very straight, the color of her skin still caught his attention, the softness and the scent that came from her were her hallmark as a woman. If he looked in the mirror, he could see her small but very firm breasts and the outline of her figure.

Twenty years had passed since they got married, and she still retained the gift of youth. To know her age, one had to look at her ID, there was no other way. The most adventurous who dared to try to guessdid not go beyond 34.

Time had passed, and he could say that he had the life he had planned and wished for. In addition to Roberto Junior, they had a daughter, Fiorella Patricia, a couple of years after their son. They were both beautiful in childhood, and now that they were two young people, they had entered university. Roberto Junior had enrolled in architecture and Fiorella in graphic design.

In his professional life, he could not complain either. He had advanced as an architecture professor and was recognized as an academic authority at the age of 45. He was on track to become the Dean and why not the Rector of the University in due time. As he downsized the architecture firm after inheriting from his father, he only carried out two or three high-value projects that provided him with high profits and prestige. This allowed him to keep the other architects in the firm and continue in the environment that corresponded to the Mendy's. Regarding the rest of the inheritance, with good financial decisions, he had managed to multiply the value of the capital he received and continued to work in real estate in conjunction with a manager, buying, selling, and renting the properties left by the previous two Roberto Mendy's.

As far as life was concerned, Roberto was satisfied. He had led a quiet, serene life without any ups and downs, with a established daily routine in which he enjoyed his wife, children, and the necessary time for recreation.

He usually taught classes in the morning, so he decided to take the children to the school located very close to the house in the same El Poblado neighborhood. He shared quality time with them and could get involved in their concerns and adolescent anxieties.

He then continued to the University, always taking the first classes so that he could be at the Firm after 2 pm and stay there until 5 pm. He would arrive home and go to the sauna, followed by his daily workout without fail. This allowed him to be in perfect physical shape and healthy. At 45 years old, he didn't have an extra gram of fat and had an impeccable and enviable athletic figure, as he used to say among friends and over drinks, he had to be on par with his wife.

Golf was a part of his life, as it had been for his father and grandfather. He was an excellent player with a very low handicap and played on Saturdays and Sundays. On Saturdays, he played in the afternoon between 5 and 7 pm so that he could have time for any commitments with Isabella or the children. On Sundays, he played very early, depending on the time he woke up, but always around 6 am.

Usually, his friends invited him on Saturdays to stay with them and have a Scotch or wine, but he only took one drink and then went back home to have dinner with Isabella and the children. Besides, he was not the type who liked alcohol.

Now that their children were 20 and 18 years old, it was very difficult to establish that Roberto and Isabella were the parents when they went out together. They looked like a group of four friends or two couples going out to dinner or to have fun, and both women loved it. It was an incentive for him to maintain his lifestyle of sharing quality family time, both for staying in shape and for maintaining the same style of life.

He could notcomplain, and he didn't, but when he remembered his childhood, he felt the pain of the loneliness he had to endure due to his mother's orphanhood and his father's absence, always busy building a real estate empire that he never got to enjoy and never shared with anyone. Instead, he had managed to balance, or rather tilt, the scale towards family attention rather than business and material goods production. He did not regret planning his life and executing it as planned, the results spoke for themselves.

Regarding Isabella, the marriage had also worked out well for her. Although she had doubts at first and even thought that his unusual impulse to propose after trying to distance himself from her, in the midst of the news that she was pregnant, would result in a disaster with divorce included and all the consequences for the children, things stabilized,and she proved to be exactly what he had thought: a very capable and intelligent woman.

She perfectly represented her role as a society lady and had never made a mistake at any reception, neither in the way she dressed nor in the way she treated friends and acquaintances. In short, she seemed to have been born for it.

Love had come slowly, gently, through the way they treated each other, the respect and consideration they had for each other. It was a sweet, serene, accommodating love, sufficient to lead the life they lived. It was stability.

For Roberto, Isabella was a breath of fresh air. Over the years, shehad not changed her way of being and always had a smile on her lips and a witty remark to make. While he was the serious and circumspect one in the relationship, she was the one in the middle of the parties, jokes, and pranks. Everyone wanted to gather with them, but Roberto knew that the main reason was to spend a pleasant evening with her witty remarks.

-Are you getting ready to go out? Shall we dine out tonight?- he asked, interrupting his contemplation of her uncovered torso. She slowly pulled up the robe that had fallen to her waist and turned around.

-No, Roberto, how can we go out to dinner tonight if we leave early tomorrow on the first flight to Bogotá?

-It wasn't an invitation;it was a question. But yes, you're right.

-On the bed, I took out what I think you should pack in your suitcase in case you want to check it before storing it. It's there. Look carefully so you don't have to go out and buy anything and then waste time on it.

He looked at her and then turned to the bed. All his clothes were selected by type and in small bundles, separated by space and by color. Hedid not need to review it further. In the 20 years they had been traveling together, he had never put in or taken out anything that she had arranged before.

He pretended to review the clothes, but he was really thinking about the trip to Bogotá that hedid notagree with. It was an important test for their marriage. He could not remember evaluating the quality or intensity of the love that bound them. It is amazing how one can be married for twenty years and not stop to think if that person who has been by your side all this time is the right person.That iswhy this trip they were embarking on the next morning gave him a sense of fear and uncertainty.

Isabella looked at him while he pretended to review the clothes she had selected for the trip to Bogotá. She was sure he would not take anything out or add anything, but she had to let him check the contents of the suitcase. It could happen that one day he would disagree with her selection. Itdid nothappen, but there could always be a first time.

She thought about how quickly these twenty years had passed. It all started that day when she found out she was pregnant until she told him in the mall cafeteria. She went through real moments of anguish, looking back, not knowing how she could feel that she could continue alone without the support of the father of the child she was expecting.

Now she did not regret what she did or the decision she made to accept marriage with Roberto without having properly dated. They went from fifteen to twenty days of intensity, then a silence of two or three weeks and the news of the pregnancy.

They were very young, Roberto wasalone, and she was far from her parents, they had to decide with very little information about each other and with very little experience. But everything had turned out well.

She went to live with him a few days later, in a mansion built by his grandfather, meaning it had three generations of Mendy's. When she arrived at the house, Roberto was starting a renovation, and shedid not know if that was good for the pregnancy, but she collaborated with him on the design and had the opportunity to contribute several ideas so that the house would be to the liking of both. Roberto let her make those decisions, which she loved at first.

With the pregnancy underway, the preparations for the wedding and the renovation, she had to leave university, but it did not weigh on her so much because she got involved in almost all the architecture firm's projects. She realized that her part was in creation, in imagination, she could see the designs and explain them to Roberto and the other architects, they took notes and drew them, when they met to see the results, the models looked much like how she imagined them. That filled her with satisfaction.

She gave birth to Roberto Junior at just nineteen years old, and two years later the girl was born. When she was barely twenty-one, she had finished having children and thought about going back to university, but then she quickly got used to the life of Medellin's society, the gym, the club, friends, and the two international trips they made each year. At first, they did it without the children, and then they traveled as a family of four. There were always one or two opportunities where Roberto and she could go out without the children, but those were very short trips.

Furthermore, there was always her participation in the architecture firm's projects that gave her satisfaction to see how her creativity was economically fruitful and taken into account by the professionals who worked for them.

The way she had lived these years allowed her to maintain her fitness, her friends always asked her how she managed to look so young and in good physical shape. She was tall, her silhouette still that of a woman in her twenties and her features did not betray that she was nearing forty. Her small breasts remained firm, and her complexion was hard but with soft and smooth skin. Her long black hair down to her waist and her very light brown complexion helped her to look like an exotic beauty in Medellin's society.

The truth was that Roberto was also in good physical shape, and his French appearance with the beard he had been wearing for a few years now made the couple look spectacular. She always believed that the genetics of a woman from the Colombian coast living in a cool climate like this city contributed to the way she had preserved herself and how she looked.

Isabella took care of making life in the marriage fun and out of routine. She always planned trips abroad when the children had school vacations and internal trips in the country whenever possible, during weekends or national holidays.

Birthday celebrations and Christmas and carnival festivities were celebrated with parties at home or at the club. She made sure that Roberto's nostalgia and retreat did not show in the daily life of the family or friends.

The trips abroad were always her dream as a young woman, and now that she was able to carry them out, she did so meticulously, choosing destination by destination to enjoy to the fullest and obtain the culture and knowledge she desired from each city, town, and country she visited. This allowed her to complement her creativity with ideas from European or Asian countries that kept her at the forefront of Medellin's society and helped her make important contributions to the architecture firm.

The children were a separate matter. If in the first few days when she was alone in the apartment her father rented for her in Medellin, she had the initial thoughts that many young students often have when unexpectedly becoming pregnant, those thoughts disappeared entirely, and the conviction that those children were hers emerged. Roberto had only contributed the seed that procreated them; the rest belonged to her, and she raised them that way.

All decisions on how to dress, where to study, what to eat, when to go out, friends, everything, in general, passed through her supervision and approval.

Roberto was always with them, present in the house, during outings, recreation, and trips. He was always there with them, but he felt distant, like he was observing, watching them grow under the mother's tutelage. He was like an essential decoration, but a decoration, nonetheless. His children had never expressed their feelings about this, but there was a tacit understanding of the situation among the four of them, or at least, that's how she understood it.

The two children were very similar to their father. Roberto Jr. had inherited the temperaments of his grandfather and great-grandfather, according to what Roberto told her - he was an entrepreneur, restless, business-minded, and hyperactive, which didn't correspond to the tranquility, passivity, and lethargy in which his father lived.

Fiorella had European features with the vivacity and charms of Isabella. She was very proud of her two children. Having them early helped her to balance the ups and downs of marriage and to stay active.

The move of those children to Bogotá was another thing. She had to talk to each one and convince them that it was the best thing for their future and their career. Roberto Jr. was studying architecture like all the Mendy's He had the desire to become a project developer like his grandparents and continue the work his father had stopped. Fiorella was studying graphic design with the intention of participating in fashion and kinetic art, which was one of her greatest abilities.

Bogotá could give them a broader perspective in their professional careers and open up wider social and political connections than Medellin. With those connections, they could return to the hometown later to pursue their professions with the support of their family. Roberto disagreed with this move from the first day it was mentioned, so she started by talking and convincing the children first that it was best for both of them. When they spoke with Roberto, the decision had already been made.

It was a very difficult step for her. Separating from both children at the same time opened up an immense wound in her heart, but it was the best thing for them, and when they returned as a man and a woman, they would have time to share and move their lives forward.

Roberto and Fiorella would move into one of the apartments their father had in Bogotá. They had to wait for the tenants to vacate and do several renovations works to make them comfortable.

The apartment was located in one of the best areas of the city, had 4 bedrooms, more than 300 square meters, 4 parking spaces, and room for escorts and drivers. Roberto tried to delay the work until she intervened very surreptitiously to ensure that everything was finished on time, and the children arrived in time for the start of classes at the university.

As always, he had taken care of the tickets and the transfers to the apartment. They were flying on a Tuesday and would be back in Medellin on Saturday morning, when they would return alone, perhaps for the first time in 20 years. A new life would begin for them, different.

-Everything is in order, I'm going to put it in the small suitcase, I think everything will fit. I'll close it and then take a shower so we can have dinner,- Roberto said.

-Check it well because we're going to be away for 5 days, and the small suitcase can ruin all the clothes. Please take precautions,- she replied.

-You're right, as always, when it comes to suitcases, I'll use the bigger one then,- he said, walking to the closet, approaching and giving her a very light kiss on the back. She turned and looked at him, he thought he saw some sadness or nostalgia in her gaze, but a moment later the thought disappeared.

-I'm always right, Roberto,- she smiled and said in the distance.

-Uhm, it's true,- he muttered already in the closet.

Roberto took a shower and changed. When he came out, she was already dressed to go downstairs, wearing black shorts that were not too tight but showed off her figure, a beige short-sleeved shirt almost to the waistband of the shorts, and black sneakers. Her hair was tied up in a bun, and she wore no makeup. Dressed that way, she looked almost like a teenager, slim, tall, and carefree.

-You look very young dressed like that.

-For God's sake, Roberto, I'm not wearing anything out of the ordinary. You're like my friends, I feel like I'm going back in time.

-Sometimes I think that, and I believe I have to get rid of the beard in order to keep going out with you, people will think I'm your dad.

-Well, you know what, it's not a bad idea – she told him, not liking the beard – and burst out laughing because he didn't know why she said it.

-Do I look old to you when I'm with you?

-No, honey, just stay still, you'll look better little by little.

-I don't understand you, Isabella, talk to me seriously, for God's sake.

-Why so serious? Let it go, don't think too much about it – and she kept looking at him in a mocking tone.

-No, Isabella, sometimes I don't understand you, there's no way of knowing what you're really thinking, let's just leave it at that and go have dinner, I'm hungry. Have the kids come down?

-What kids? I just found out there are kids in this house, did you have more children and not tell me?

-Oh no, no, let's go downstairs.

She went down the stairs laughing and not knowing how Roberto, after 20 years, had not gotten used to her way of thinking and speaking. Serious things were not her strong suit, life was too heavy when people took it seriously, and she always preferred to look at the fun, soft, and rosy side of things happening around her. When they got to the dining room, the two children were already waiting, sitting and chatting merrily.

Roberto stared at them, unable to believe that this was the last dinner together, well, not the last one because they would come back for vacations and holidays, but at least it was the last one they would have as a family in the same nucleus, hedid notknow how to define it, he didn't feel good about this move.

In addition, when they notified him, it wasn't a consultation, it was a notification, they had already decided it with his mother, they didn't take him into account, and they didn't care much about his opinion. He felt resentment, he couldn't channel it towards his children, so there was only one person he could blame for all of this: Isabella. He had protested enough but it didn't do any good, so he decided to go along with it at least to spend the last few days together in harmony.

-Mom, I finished packing my suitcase, but I'm still missing a lot of things, I'm thinking we should send some of the things I want to take as cargo.

-Fiorella, we already sent a lot of very large boxes, we'll have to buy you a truck to make weekly trips just for you, girl. You know what? Leave all that here and if you need anything, either buy it or we'll send it little by little, how about that?

-Yeah, you're right, I'll just buy everything new.

-Look, girl, that consumerist mindset doesn't seem like the best response to me,- interrupted Roberto, and Fiorella and Isabella winked at each other and laughed, causing Roberto to fall back into their games.

-I don't want to take anything else with me, not even my suitcase. It's not like I'm going to buy anything,- said Roberto Junior, looking at his dad. -But everything I have is more than boring to me. Besides, I don't know what I'm going to find there, so I prefer to have as little as possible.- His tone of voice and reasoning sounded like that of a young person who was older and more mature.

-Whatever you say, daddy,- his mother responded.

They continued to talk very animatedly while they dined. Roberto gradually let go of his nostalgia and bad mood and joined in the conversation, trying not to fall into Fiorella and her mother's games. Roberto Junior asked about properties in Bogotá and how they could make better use of them, which houses they could remodel to sell at a higher price, and if they had any land to develop.

Roberto tried to answer as honestly as possible without giving away all the exact information but without seeming evasive. That son had turned out just like his father and grandfather, and he could not find a way to communicate how that behavior had hurt the family so much.

They went to bed early because their flight was in the morning. They had already prepared everything and left their suitcases with the driver before going upstairs. Roberto said goodbye to each of his children in their room, as he used to do when they were little. He briefly chatted with them and then went to his room.

He found Isabella already lying on the left side of the bed, leaning on her right arm. This position made her sleep with her back to him. He went to the bathroom, freshened up, and when he returned to the bed, she was already asleep.

He lay down and started thinking about the resentment he was feeling. He didn't like these feelings towards the woman he had shared 20 years with and who had given him two children. He looked at her and felt that lately, they weren't intimate much. They were very polite when they were together, but he felt distant. Something was missing in their marriage.

Perhaps with the departure of the children, they would have the opportunity to rekindle their passion and renew their love. He fell asleep with this thought, and the resentment softened in his heart.

Isabella felt him arrive in bed, she did not move, she wasn't pretending to be asleep, she was just very still. She knew he would not try to move her or call her, that was Roberto. He wouldn't take anything she didn't offer, no matter if he desired it or not. He simply would not take the initiative if he thought she was upset, angry, distant, sad, tired, or anything else. No, he would not be that proactive person in the marriage who, with passion and fury, even without force but with conviction, rescued a bad moment in the relationship. She could go a week without looking at him or speaking to him, and he would come in and give her a kiss on the cheek and continue to the study to read or watch a movie.

He would leave for golf andwould not invite her out unless she was waiting for him dressed and ready to go to dinner or dance. A tear rolled down her face and reached the corner of her lips. It had been 20 years, and her heart was wringing, but she would not let that take away the joy of living with which she was born. She fell asleep little by little.

They got up very early, but with barely enough time for coffee and left for José Maria Córdoba, they were relatively close, and it was a journey of almost 30 minutes.

The flight was on time and very pleasant, at 6:10 a.m. the plane took off from Medellin, the flight time was approximately 50 minutes, so they were outside the airport in Bogotá at 7:45 a.m. They went to have breakfast before arriving at the apartment and settled the children into their new home before noon.

On that first day in the city, they took a nap and went to malls and supermarkets to stock up on food and complete the furniture and utensils. The women focused on clothes and decorations for the house, and the men went to electronics stores for televisions, computers, and communication and internet equipment. It was a busy day with lunch and dinner out.

The next day, Roberto had meetings with several of the administrators of the properties he had in Bogotá. He wanted to review personally and in detail the situation of each of the investments in the city and review the potential of each business. His son's insistence on doing something different or restructuring the businessdid not seem like a bad idea, only that it involved what he had avoided for all these years: raising the pressure and stress of work, the commitment to third parties, the evaluation of success and achievements. In short, a completely different lifestyle than he had planned.

Roberto Junior would join him in the afternoon after finishing his registration at the university. He always enjoyed spending time with his son, feeling that he was the continuation of the Mendy dynasty. Furthermore, he had chosen to study architecture, just like his father and grandfather, which filled him with even more pride.

Sometimes he felt like his son did not approve of the lifestyle he led. Roberto Junior was like his father and grandfather, with an exceptional initiative and work capacity. He always stood out for doing more than others, whether it was in studies, sports, or social groups. He was always the leader, directing or leading others to new ventures.

This hurt him, but he knew it was something personal. Nevertheless, he was sure that his son loved and respected him.

Roberto Junior and Fiorella formally registered at the university in the morning, had lunch on campus to begin adapting to the institute's environment in Bogotá, and in the afternoon, Roberto joined his father in meetings with administrators that interested him. He wanted to convince him to start a radical change in the way they invested and continued to expand the Mendy legacy.

Fiorella went to the apartment to fetch Isabella. The two had a lot to talk about before their parents returned to Medellin. Their lives were about to change for all four of them, and even though they had already talked a lot, she wanted to make sure everything would be okay, especially for their parents, who would be embarking on a new life away from their children.

Their mother had argued very well for why they should move and continue their careers in another city. They were both adults, ready to start an independent life, and their parents were still very young and had hardly lived alone. But she was worried about her father, who had not agreed to the move. When they returned, she didn't know how he would react, and she wanted to be sure everything would be okay. She wanted to hear it once again from her mother.

The next two days were peaceful, with the four of them strolling through the city, trying out new trendy restaurants, and meeting with people they wanted to keep in contact with for their children to develop new friendships and social and business relationships. It was the moment to introduce Roberto Junior to the most renowned architects in the country and Fiorella to people in fashion and art.

Meanwhile, Roberto was still thinking about his relationship with Isabella. This trip confirmed that they were distant, and hedid not feel the need to be with her. Perhaps he had never felt it, or maybe he was fooling himself and did feel it but found it difficult to express. He had expectations about what life would be like for the two of them alone in the house, without having to worry about the children, with all the time available to share together.

He did not want to say a word about it during the trip, as he had a higher motive of establishing the young ones in another city and thought he would have time later to address with Isabella the topics that distracted them from their relationship. Or maybe that was what he had always done, not saying a word and leaving the moment to speak and express themselves for the future. And if there was nothing to say when they spoke, or what came out was not what he or she expected to hear.

He stopped thinking and spent time with the family, after all that was what was important.

Isabella devoted herself to the children as she always did, or rather, she did it with much more intensity this time. It was going to be a good season before she saw them again, and she was not used to being away from them for long periods. They were more important in her life than she admitted to herself, but she tried to show them every day.

She made sure the apartment was prepared so that they could survive for a long season. She hired the services of the people who would assist them, interviewed them, and conducted a background check together with a professional review service. They finalized the purchase of their respective vehicles and added a non-presential escort service just to monitor them and advise them on security issues. She had to make sure they were going to be protected.

The conversation with Florella was very important. She explained the details of living with her dad and assured her that everything would be fine for both of them. They were elderly adults, and they would continue with their routine. It was the law of life that at some point, children separated from their parents.

On Saturday, everyone got up very early and said their goodbyes with hugs and attempts at suppressed sobs and tears. The taxi service arrived before sunrise, and Roberto and Isabella took the flight back to Medellin at the same time they had arrived five days earlier. The trip was also very calm, and before 11 in the morning, they were both alone at home.

They talked very little during the journey. Isabella lay down for a while and closed her eyes on the plane, and Roberto read a book by a new writer named Miguel Ángel Zeles. Both felt the weight of leaving their children, and as the plane took off and moved away, they felt how nostalgia stretched along the road between Bogotá and Medellin. They attributed each other's silence to the farewell and the pain.

In the taxi, they did not talk much either, and upon arriving, only routine things were discussed, such as how they had found the house. Isabella said she wanted to take a nap because she was tired and had an appointment at the beauty salon at 4 p.m. in the afternoon, and Robertoreplied that he would go to his usual Saturday afternoon golf game. He went for a run for a while and then to the gym.

He had only eaten a sandwich he made himself in the kitchen anddid not hear any more noise in the house until he saw Isabella's truck leaving at almost 3:50 p.m. from the study, he realized the time and also headed to the Club Campestre for his golf game, which was less than 10 minutes away from his location.

Today, the president of the architecture faculty and the architect who managed the Mendy firm would accompany him. They were regulars on Saturdays, so he already knew that after the game, they would invite him for a Scotch, which was never just one.

The game always started at 5 p.m. so he had enough time to have a coffee and chat with the managers of one of the two restaurants at the Club. His companions arrived, and they began playing.

They finished playing around 6:45 p.m. when it was already getting dark and went straight to shower in their cubicles and then to La Ronda Bar, an English-style sports pub bar. They started with their favorite Scotch and began discussing the move of Roberto's children. The two friends had been involved from the beginning, since Roberto married Isabella, and were honestly interested in the future of the young people, especially Roberto, who was studying architecture, like all of them.

He explained to them the reasons and the strategy they wanted to follow so that their children could develop in their professional careers, but above all in the societies of the two main cities in the country. While they continued to talk, he remembered that Isabella was alone at home, that she had gone to the beauty salon and was probably waiting for him like every Saturday, dressed and ready for dinner, or maybe she had come up with something different or bought tickets for a concert, and he had accepted more of the regular drink that he always shared with his friends.

He felt a sudden urgency, abruptly cut the conversation, apologized, and headed towards the parking lot. Hedid not know if he had done it unconsciously or if he was trying to avoid being alone with Isabella. He felt remorse and a little guilt.

He drove the 4 kilometers that separated the house from the club thinking that today he was starting a new life and he was not starting it very well. Hedid not know how things would be from now on, but in order for things to improve, he would have to do his part. Maybe all these years had passed too quickly between raising the children and taking care of the details to lead a peaceful and harmonious life as he always thought.

He arrived home and the lights were not on. Isabella's truck was not in the parking lot but almost blocking the entrance. He drove in very slowly so as not to scratch or bump into the sidemirrors and was able to park his vehicle. It all seemed very strange, both the truck and the lights. When he got out of the car, he could see that the light in the first room was on, giving a sad and dark reflection to the rest of the house.

He entered through the kitchen and put down his golf bag, leaned it against the entrance and turned on the lights as he walked into the house. He headed to the room with the light on, thinking he would find Isabella there.

The feeling of guilt and remorse gave way to anxiety as a result of the darkness of the house and Isabella's truck blocking the entrance. He did not want to think that something bad had happened or that intruders had entered the house. That would not happen with the security services and surveillance they had contracted, and the additional security of the gated community. Nothing had ever happened there in the many years they had been living in that house since his grandfather built it.

He was relieved when he saw Isabella. Nothing negative had happened as he had feared. She was standing with her back to him, looking out the window towards the garden, and turned around when he entered the room. He found her exactly as he had thought she would be, and the feeling of guilt overwhelmed him again, this time with much greater force.

She was stunning she was wearinga white jumpsuitthat hugged her body at the waist and torso, highlighting her perfect silhouette and accentuating the beauty of her hips and breasts. The jumpsuit was completely closed in the front and had a neckline that went halfway down her back. Thejumpsuit's boots fell in a bell shape along her legs, and the nude-colored high-heeled shoes stood out against the white of thejumpsuit. She had her long hair down, extremely straight and held at the temple by two small hooks that were not visible and made her well-made-up and outlined face stand out. She was beautiful as he had rarely seen her, or as he had always seen her.

He felt a punch in the stomach, he was late, and they had surely missed some reservation that Isabella had made. He deduced this from the seriousness with which she was looking at him. He did not let her start talking. She was not usually so formal in her speech or her gaze.

-Excuse me, Isa, I'm really sorry. When we were on our way here, the boys started asking me about our kids and how we had left them in Bogota and all that, and time got away from me.- His words were not coming out in order. He, who was always so precise and calm, felt embarrassed to be late and find her so well-dressed. Most likely, they had missed out on something well planned. -I had two Scotches instead of the one I usually have with them. I'll go up and change quickly. You'll see.- He gestured to go back in the direction of the room.

-Don't go, Roberto, we don't have much time,- Isabella replied.

-But it's just a moment. You know I can change very quickly if I want to. Besides, I already showered at the club. I just need to put on something appropriate for your elegance, and we'll go.- He didn't ask where they were going. Maybe she had already told him, and he didn't want to make the situation more serious than it already was.

She gestured with her hand for him to stop and come closer, still looking serious. There was no smile, as she usually had, and no reproachful gesture, as he was expecting. Only a serious, even tender, gaze. Isabella took a step towards him and stopped.

-I just want to talk to you, Roberto. There's not much I need to tell you. Don't go, there's not much time,- she continued.

-I don't understand, Isabella. I've already apologized for being late, and I've told you what kept me. I also said I'd change quickly. What do you want to talk about?- He was speaking very slowly. His brain wasn't processing the scene. He had never had a moment like this with her before. It was either his mind or his fear of being alone that made him see things that weren't happening or weren't real. -Let me change, and then we'll talk. Okay?- He offered again.

-Roberto, I'm leaving,- she began. Her features saddened, tears filled her eyes, and her lips trembled.-I'm going to the airport.

He stared at her, they hadn't talked about any trip, he was sure of that. There was no mention of it, no suitcase, no preparation. She had not told him thedestination; they had not discussed it. In fact, they had not even talked about what they would do once they returned from Bogotá. They had just arrived from a trip. Hedid not know what to think, his mind was in chaos. He decided to look for the answer where he thought he would find it, in her eyes. Hedid not like what he saw.

-But we haven't talked about any trip,- he began to say, but she interrupted him.

-No, Roberto, we haven't talked about any trip. In fact, we haven't talked about many things for a long time. I'm going on this trip alone, well, not alone. For all these years, I've waited for you to look at me, to see me as the woman that I am. That 19-year-old girl who gave herself to you and came to live in this house with so much hope. I know we didn't fall in love like many other people do, but I always wished that love would grow between us. God knows how hard I tried to make that happen, but it never did. Instead, with time, you got used to your quiet and passive life. You had me, you had the children, you had financial security, and you had no challenges in life. But you also didn't have the spark and passion that my soul needs. Forgive me for not speaking up earlier. Maybe we could have had a chance, but I stayed quiet, and you didn't bring up the topic either.- She paused. The lump in her throat wouldn't let her continue, and tears threatened to ruin her makeup.

Roberto tried to interrupt her several times, like when she said she wouldn't be traveling alone. Then who would she be traveling with, a friend? Was she going on a trip with her friends? When would she come back? Or when she said they didn't fall in love like other people, yes, at some point he had thought the same thing. But now, in this precise moment, he realized that he was very much in love. She was the love of his life. He thought about interrupting her and telling her, but he didn't. He didn't say a word during the pause. She looked at him and continued.

-I have to be honest with you because that's how we've treated each other in everything we've done together, except in our love relationship. The divorce papers are in the envelope in the dining room. I'm not asking for anything material, the fortune you have is from your family and I've saved some of what you paid me for my work at the Firm. The copy of the key of the truck that I will leave at the airport is also there, and inside the compartment, I will leave the ticket to exit. I'm leaving the country with someone whose name you will know in due course. She couldn't contain the tears any longer and they flowed freely while she continued speaking.-I confess that I was unfaithful to you, with all the pain in my soul. It started as a friendship in which I confided in you about my life and ended up involved and in love. I'm telling you not to hurt you, but to make you understand that this is not a decision made lightly or a tantrum to make you react. There is no turning back, and the decisions have already been made. I was on the verge of doing this some time ago, but there was no one else. I don't know if it would have worked out, maybe it would have, but I didn't have the courage. The kids were little and needed me.

-Isabella, my God, I don't even know what to say to you, I'm speechless, I don't know what to say,- Roberto rambled incoherently. He really didn't know what to say or think. He couldn't form a coherent sentence. What could he do? If he begged her to stay, he would make a fool of himself. She was already dressed to leave for the airport. If he reacted violently to the infidelity, he would regret it for the rest of his life. He was anything but violent. If he stayed silent, he would be admitting that she was right, but what could he say to convince her to stay and talk, to give him the chance to fix what he hadn't done in these years?

-Don't say anything, it would be more painful for both of us. It hurts me, even if you don't believe me now or later, but it has hurt me for a long time. If you haven't noticed, it's because of the way I am, but the pain has been there for 20 years without knowing if you ever loved me.

-Can you at least tell me who you're going with?- he regretted asking as soon as he finished the sentence.

She looked at him with pain, shook her head, and started to walk away. She passed by his side, looked at him with sadness, but also with the same tenderness as when she arrived at the house and saw her looking out the window. She put her hand on his shoulder, squeezed it, and continued on. She picked up her purse from the table adjacent to the door and left.

He saw her walking slowly towards the door without turning, he stood in front of the same window where he had spotted her and followed her slow movements as she got into the truck. He could see how her gaze scanned the entire house, the garden, the parking lot, looking at everything from top to bottom. She got in and rested her forehead on the steering wheel. There was a time when Roberto thought she would get out, run back, and enter the house again. She put the key in the ignition, turned it and started the engine. He thought he felt a reflection of her gaze resting on his eyes, he didn't know if it was his imagination or if it really happened, but for a long time, it was the only memory he kept of her in his mind.

Roberto never knew how long he had been looking through the window, nor how long his mind was blank, nor how long he waited to see the truck lights come back through the gate. When he regained his sense of connection between his body and mind, he was sitting on the floor, leaning against the wall under the window. The first rays of sunlight were beginning to enter,and the house looked opaque with reddish and orange flashes. He had not slept, he was sure he had not slept all night, but he hardly rememberedanything. One of his arms was numb from leaning on it, and when he came to, he felt a sharp pain in the center of his chest andcould not hold back the tears.

He cried for hours, loudly, softly, sobbing, stopping, and starting again, he cried endlessly, as he had never done before, not even when his father died, nor when his mother died because he could not remember it. When he tried to stop, he kept crying for all the times in his life that he had avoided crying. He cried for his grandfather, his mother, his father, Isabella, his children and above all for himself.

He raised his head again and it was dark outside. It was almost the same time that Isabella had left, 24 hours had passed,and he was still lying on the floor under the window where he saw her leave. He had not drunk any water or eaten anything during that time, the last thing he had in his stomach were the two Scotches he had taken with his friends.

Hedid nothave the will to get up,hehad lost everything. Isabella had made sure to take away everything he longed for in life: a home, a wife, and children. Today he had none of that. She sent them to Bogotá and the same day they arrived, she abandoned him. He began to feel a rage that was turning into hatred towards Isabella. If he had never met her, if hehad not married her, if he had made her have an abortion like all the girls who tried to catch a man with the excuse of a child, he would have married a better woman and had children with her. Everything would be different, and he would not be feeling this horrible rage, this frenzied hatred towards that woman.

He sat up as best he could, and a stab in his head reminded him how dehydrated he must be and how long he had been on the floor. He went to the table to get his phone, remembered the kids, it was dead, so he plugged it in and turned it on. He had over 50 missed calls from Fiorella. He called her back as best he could. He tried to sound as sane and healthy as possible.

-Hello, my darling, how are you?- he asked.

-Oh my God, Daddy, how are you? Why didn't you answer? I've been calling for two days. I'm about to buy a ticket and go to Medellin.-

-But why are you saying that daughter? My phone just died, and I didn't charge it. Don't worry, I'm fine.

-Are you sure, Dad? Because I know very well what you're going through.

Roberto was left speechless. Did Fiorella know what was happening? Did Roberto Jr. know too? Did everyone know? Who else knew?

-How do you know?

-Of course, Daddy. How could I not know? Do you think all of this could happen without Mom telling us everything? We knew everything, but we thought you had already discussed it and that everything was okay. What I didn't expect was for you to disappear like that. I was very worried.

Roberto was not thinking clearly since last night. He had not been able to find the right words to talk to Isabella and had to watch her leave without being able to say anything. But this time was different. This was his daughter, he had to find the words that would be good for them. He had to protect his children'smental health, and the only way to do that was to lie, to play Isabella's game. Later, he would figure out what to do with the hatred that was growing every second for her. He fought the headache and searched for the right words.

-Yes, mom, you're right, everything is fine. Your mom and I talked everything out very civilly and we reached an agreement,- the words refused to come out in that order, he felt doubly betrayed, by Isabella and by himself. -I'm okay and nothing's wrong. I already told her that I didn't answer because my phone died, but nothing serious. I'm back online now and if you need anything or if you want to talk to your dad, just give me a call.- He didn't think or finish the next sentence.-And your mom should already bein... with...

-In Madrid with Alexander. I already spoke to her, and the trip went well. They've settled in where they're going to live for a while, while he does some work there. Okay, daddy, then I'll be at ease. A kiss and take care, okay? I love you so much.

-I love you too, my heart. Bye.

The headache was nothing compared to the feeling in his stomach. His legs buckled and he fell to the floor again. Suddenly he felt a pain all over his body, his skin burned and tingled. He imagined Isabella in the arms of Alexander Silva-Carpio, making love to him, kissing him, walking hand in hand through the streets of Madrid, sleeping in the same bed. He could not bear the pain it caused him. It wasn't pain in his soul or heart; it wasn't emotional pain; it was physical pain. Every organ, every inch of flesh hurt.

He forgot the hate that had been born just a few minutes ago and now could only remember every moment when he had felt a deep love for that woman and never told her. He never took a step to show her that he loved her. Despite what she believed about their marriage, he had fallen in love with her shortly after, and she was the love of his life.

Alexander Silva-Carpio had been his student in the first semester he taught at the University, so he met Isabella that same year. He introduced them and was even invited to the wedding. Alexander married young, also fresh out of college, with another student, but they separated in a couple of years. From there, he went to study in New York and came back with a master's degree in designing large buildings. Shortly after, he opened his own firm and became the youngest architect to win the national architecture prize. He was called for all the major private and public projects in the country, which earned him international fame. He built buildings around the world, including Dubai and exotic places, in the same 20 years that he was married to Isabella.

Alexander became the famous and wealthy architect that he should have been with his inheritance and knowledge. Well, he still had the fortune. Alexander was a frequent guest at his home gatherings, and it was always a success to have him with the other friends.

A week had passed, and it was already Saturday. He did not go to the usual golf game, nor to the university. He had not left the house in those 7 days. He spent the time tormented with shame, with a lot of shame. He did not want to go out to face his friends and acquaintances, so they would not ask him about Isabella, so he would not have to give explanations, simply because he did not have any.

That was the biggest shame, he felt so ashamed of himself, he did not know how to face it, he did not know what to do, he had no one to talk to, he did not know how to reason. He had buried what he felt all the time deep in his heart, he could not talk to anyone or express his feelings.

He had a wonderful woman by his side, and he did not know how to keep her, the children he longed for so he could share his love with them, he was sure he hadn't fully shown them the unrestricted love he felt for them. What the hell was wrong with him that he was so messed up inside that he seemed dead inside.

Another week passed and he sent his resignation to the university, he would not go anymore. What good was the prestige of being a professor if he had no one to share it with? Fiorella called him every day and every day he composed himself and spoke to her in a joking tone, only to end up in the self-esteem crisis that was attacking him.

If he could know or remember at what moment he lost Isabella, at what moment she decided to leave him, at what moment everything cooled between them, when she stopped feeling when they made love, when she started to be unfaithful to him, and that was when the physical pain returned,and the skin seemed to peel off in pieces.

In the third week, his intelligent man's brain told him that he had to do something, that he had to seek help, he could not do it alone, he was not functioning, he just saw himself falling and falling deeper into an abyss that had no end, every time deeper, and when this happened, the pain became more unbearable. He searched for a therapist on the internet. He went to three. He stayed with the first one, a woman.

He spent 9 months in treatment with the therapist, they became friends in the end. She never officially discharged him, but gradually he regained the desire to live and the lost confidence. He put things in their place and events in the right perspective. It was not easy; it was very painful because he had to recognize and see things that were very internal and not in the light, things that no one had taught him and that he didnot want orcould not see in the midst of the pain they caused.

He learned that humans respond to universal laws of love and loyalty to which we are bound, and that when we violate thoselaws,we can spend a lifetime without finding a solution to our problems, hurting ourselves, but also hurting the beings we are supposed to love. We hurt them unintentionally because we are like amputated from that ability to look at the correct order of the position that our loved ones play in our life. But we also hurt ourselves and them when we hold on too tightly to that love and loyalty without looking at the fact that each person around us has a role that we must respect and maintain.

Roberto understood that his problem came from denying the love he had for his father, from denying the pride and respect he felt for the immense work he did, from putting the blame on his father for losing his mother. Hecould not forgive that his father had abandoned him when he did not have a mother.

He understood that none of that was his father's fault, that his father loved him as much as he loved his children and gave him everything he could because that was all he had received. He understood that not even the word -forgiving- his father should have passed through his mind or his soul because he had nothing to forgive his father for. Children do not have to forgive their parents; gratitude and love are what children can feel towards their parents. They gave them life, and that is enough.

Roberto also understood that he had set aside the pride of being a Mendy, and that had weakened him as a person and as a man. The greatest strength we have comes from our ancestors, and to the extent that we deny their legacy, we lose our strengths.

A year after starting therapy, he reopened the Mendy Construction Company in Medellin and took charge of it. He decided to call Roberto Junior and put him in charge of the restructuring of the businesses in Bogotá. He needed to give him the confidence he had denied him as a result of not having it himself.

He went to the banks and financiers and convinced them to make the necessary investment for a complex of buildings on the land his father had left on the outskirts of the city, which was the largest construction project in the department in recent years. He contracted with the government through his many relationships for the construction of roads and highways and employed a staff of 30 architects for the firm.

In summary, at 46 years old, Roberto Mendy was being reborn, the third of the dynasty, the best prepared of all, and the most aware of what the strength of an ancestral heritage of entrepreneurs and builders can be.

Regarding Isabella, he obtained her phone number through Fiorella, he asked for it with all responsibility, it was a single conversation that he needed to have with her.

He reached her in New York, greeted her, and explained what he wanted to talk to her about. He asked if it bothered her, and she said no, so he proceeded. He told her what he had gone through, omitting the painful details, but basically how he found the answers. He told her how his feelings had been blocked by the mistaken ideas he had of his father and his father's relationship with his mother. He apologized for leading her into a marriage with an absent husband, an absent father, a person who did not communicate with himself. He told her that he was not yet healthy but was working to be at any time, and if he did not succeed, he would keep working. He said that there was no deadline and no end to the relentless search for true peace and harmony, which was nothing other than being alive and being able to love fully. He told her that she was only a victim of a victim.

When he hung up the phone, he cried for the last time over his lost marriage.

With the busy life he was leading professionally, there was no time for university, although his resignation was never accepted. But it had been an advantage to separate himself from that sedentary life because with so many meetings and work he had; he wouldn't have had time to pay much attention. What he did was guarantee Fiorella's job in Medellin, in case she ever wanted to return to her hometown, and he bought an art gallery, one of the best in the city.

He saw his children once a month when he went to Bogota between visiting and work trips.

It was at the Gallery that he met Eleanor, a very young woman of 28 years, very intelligent and cultured, who was already the curator of the Gallery at her age.

The first time he saw her was when the gallery staff was notified that they had a new owner. She approached and graciously offered to resign from her position as if it were a political position, as Roberto saw it. But then she explained to him that it was very common because the new owner might want to redefine the purpose of the Gallery.

But that was not the case, and Roberto explained it to her. From then on, what everyone saw as a boss-employee relationship began, but at his age, and now recovered from his trauma and separation from Isabella, Roberto once again felt the need for the warmth of a woman in his life, in his bed, and in his thoughts. But this time it would be different. This time he thought he would choose with all his senses in place, with all the passion bursting from his skin, and with all the strength of a man. And he hadchosen Eleanor.

He invited her to lunch several times to discuss work matters and spent a lot of time at the Gallery once he was free from the construction company or the firm. Every time he returned from Bogotá, he would stop by with the excuse of giving her messages from Fiorella, as if theydid not talk on the phone. Eleanor noticed the deference and did nothide her reciprocal liking.

During one of their lunches, Roberto opened up to her:

- Do you know where your name comes from?

- You know I do; you know where I work, don't you?

- Of course, I do – he laughed out loud – but don't you think it's not a coincidence? You know, I've learned, being a bit older now, that coincidences don't exist. Doesn't it surprise you that Eleanor has its origin in the ancient French name Aliénor?

- And what does it matter that my name comes from a French one? – she replied, squinting her eyes.

-That I descend from the French - it was another Roberto with total confidence and even funny.

-And who should I thank?, because you descend from the French and I have a French name? Can you enlighten me?

-Well, I imagine some god like Ogmios was the one who gave names, but you can thank whoever you want, as long as you agree with me that your name and my ancestors come from the same place.

-Hahaha, very funny.

-And the best part is that the meaning of Aliénor is-Ardor of the Sun-so...

-Uhum uhum - she interrupted him, dead of laughter - Mr. Mendy, you seem to be going too far.

-No, on the contrary, Eleanor, I've been respectful for a long time, but there comes a time when things have to be said - she began to blush, unlike Isabella, Eleanor was a very fair-skinned woman, with light brown hair and greenish amber eyes, which according to Roberto changed color depending on her mood. She was tall, very thin, almost the same size as him, and had a generous bust that contrasted with her thinness - at this point, I can't keep quiet about what I feel, it's not honest with you and it's not honest with me either.

-But be careful with what you say Roberto - she replied with a sigh and almost no voice.

-Yes, precisely, that's what I want, to be careful, to be able to take care of a possible relationship with you - he chose his words carefully - at my age, you'll know that I have no doubts about what I want, you know my position and my marital status, I'm free, I have no ties and no deadlines. These last few months with you have confirmed what I feel and what I want.

-Yes, but you know my status too - she replied after a while meditating on her answer, looking him straight in the eyes.

-Yes, I know and I respect it, I just ask that you consider me, that you give me a chance to reach you, that you give me the opportunity to show you what I feel and that what I feel is serious, it's great and it's very beautiful, that you are the only woman in my life that I have chosen, that you are the first one that I intend to pursue, taking the initiative myself, it sounds kind of weird coming from a man of my age, but you know my story - Roberto had shared part of his therapy with her, because she was a very intelligent woman.

-Yes, I know - she took some time to answer again - and I don't know what to say, what you're telling me flatters me, yes, it flatters me a lot, but you know that I'm committed, I've been with my boyfriend for 5 years and...

-Don't give me an answer yet, it's not necessary, I'm not asking for it, no, don't answer. I just want what I told you, don't close the door on me, consider that every time we go out, you're not going out with your boss or a friend, but with a man who is in love with you and if you allow it, can love you like no one else would, that I am in fullness of my feelings, that without wanting to praise myself more than allowed, without being a spiritual being ascended, I am in full knowledge of my limitations and I am working to be better every day, to be able to share with you a full and healthy love.

-I haven't closed the door on you, we're here, we both know what's happening, you're not indifferent to me, and you've noticed that, I just need time to make a decision.

-Don't worry about me, I have the time that God has appointed for me to have on my part there's no rush and contact with you and your company are enough for me, for now, to feel that I'm on the right path.

-For now? What does that mean? She laughed.

They continued talking, he took her back to the Gallery and they said goodbye with a soft kiss on the cheek that lasted an eternity, he felt the softness of her skin and she breathed in his scent of a man in love, they both closed their eyes as if it werea kiss of love.

ABOUT THE AUTHOR

Fabio H Soto Salom is a Certified Public Accountant in Venezuela. He worked for many years at an important accounting firm in the country and retired in 2017 when he moved to Miami, in the state of Florida, USA. While he was working at this formal firm, hepublished a book under the pseudonym Miguel Ángel Zeles, and also wrote verses and phrases on the Instagram page, @palabrasdemaz.

Today, that page is in his own name and the pseudonym has disappeared. This does not mean he can't write something else under this fiction, but for now, the path is open for him to continue with his own creations.

www.ingramcontent.com/pod-product-compliance
Lightning Source LLC
LaVergne TN
LVHW010611100826
845148LV00014B/2924

* 9 7 8 1 7 3 6 1 9 9 1 5 2 *